the CLEARING

A mystery

Dorothy Reynolds Miller

The CLEARING

The CLEARING

A Mystery

Dorothy Reynolds Miller

A Jean Karl Book

Atheneum Books for Young Readers

Atheneum Books for Young Readers

An imprint of Simon & Schuster

Children's Publishing Division

1230 Avenue of the Americas

New York, New York 10020

Text copyright © 1996 by Dorothy Miller

Book design by Ethan Trask

The text of this book is set in Weiss 11pt.

First Edition

Printed in the United States of America

10 9 8 7 6 5 4 3 2 1

Library of Congress Cataloging-in-Publication Data

Miller, Dorothy Reynolds.

The clearing : a mystery / Dorothy Reynolds Miller.—1st ed.

p.   cm.

"A Jean Karl book."

Summary: While spending the summer with her cousins in rural
Pennsylvania, eleven-year-old Amanda becomes involved with a
long-ago tragedy that has impacted the lives of many local residents.

ISBN 0-689-80997-2

[1. Cousins—Fiction. 2. Death—Fiction.] I. Title.

PZ7.M61265Cl   1996

[Fic]—dc20   95-49076

The
CLEARING

A Mystery

Dorothy Reynolds Miller

A Jean Karl Book

Atheneum Books for Young Readers

Dedicated to my parents,
Pearl and Bill Reynolds,
with love.

The CLEARING

PROLOGUE

There's an article about Charles. "Well known local illustrator," he's called.

Can it have been so long ago, that summer in the clearing?

CHAPTER ONE

Chad and Jessie are thinking of moving to Minneapolis, halfway across the country, practically the other side of the world! At least that's what it seems like to me,.

Chad and Jessie are my parents. We've lived in Stump, Pennsylvania, for all of my life. Eleven years.

I say the word over and over to myself, "Minneapolis." It has five syllables! That's what's wrong with it. I've always been able to tell everyone where I live with just one syllable, Stump. I don't want to have to say Minn-e-a-po-lis! Or would that be, Minn-e-ap-ol-is? Minneapolis might be a fine place, but it has four syllables too many. Stump is short and simple. That's what I like. That's what suits me.

I'm especially negative after Jessie mumbles something about Minnesota winters being a lot longer and colder than Pennsylvania winters. I've just survived a long winter, and I'm too happy with warmth, openness, green leaves and flowers to think about any kind of winter, especially one that is end-less and far away.

Several weeks go by while they dither around thinking about it.

Then one Sunday they talk it over with Aunt Sally and Uncle Cliff. I miss most of the conversation because I'm out playing badminton with my cousin, Elinore. But after I win seventeen games, she refuses to play anymore, so we go in, and Chad announces that they've decided to try Minneapolis for the summer. His company is opening a new branch there, and if he likes it there he can make a permanent transfer. If not he can still come back to Stump. They're going to check it out. I'm going to stay with Aunt Sally. If they decide to move to Minneapolis after they get out there and see what it's like, they'll send for me.

A summer at Aunt Sally's! A whole summer with Elinore! I'm excited. But I'm also worried. Elinore is just plain excited. She starts hopping up and down and screaming, "Amanda, Amanda!" She's screaming all the things we can do.

And I must admit, it does sound like fun. Except that I've never been away from home for more than a night or two. And for all of my life there's just been the three of us, Chad, Jessie, and me. They've never gone anywhere alone, and I'm not sure they can manage.

I think about it for several days, and then I decide, a sum-mer might not be too long for them to be alone.

Aunt Sally's house is almost thirty miles from Stump. It sits with eleven other houses in a clearing that's surrounded by woods. The houses just seem like they were plopped there by someone who decided growing houses was easier than growing corn.

The place doesn't have a name, except that the road that goes past it is called the Lake View Hill Road. There's no lake, no hill and no view. Lucky there's a road.

We've visited there a lot, so I know most of the kids, but I've never stayed overnight. The best part of the clearing is the woods. I love woods. I've read all the books our school library has about Indians, and one of my favorite things is imagining that some of them are still living deep in the woods, so deep that, for all of these years since America was discovered, no one has ever found them.

Not that I'd rather live on Lake View Hill Road than in Stump. Stump is surrounded by far-off, wooded hills. But there are also shops and long streets. In Stump there is variety.

As Chad and Jessie leave I say, "I like Stump." I hope they understand what I mean. I don't want to make too strong a case for Stump in case Minneapolis is heaven on earth. But I want them to know that Minneapolis should be astonishingly magnificent if we're going to move there.

The houses in the clearing have big yards and large gardens. Not many trees. But with the whole clearing surrounded by woods, I guess no one wants more trees. They just want flowers. In the summer there are flowers everywhere, as though the people are saying, Hey, sunshine, come here, look at this open spot in the woods. There's a place here where every color can grow.

I have two other cousins, besides Elinore, who live in the

clearing on Lake View Hill Road. Uncle Dan and his kids, Nelson and Annette. Of them my favorite is Nelson. He's eleven, the same age as Elinore and me.

Mrs. Mead lives alone in the biggest, nicest house. She's two houses down from Aunt Sally. Across the street from her are the Kennedys. They have a lot of children, and they live in the smallest, most run-down house. But even in front of their house there are mounds of flowers.

A lot of kids live in the houses in the clearing. Of all of them I like Cynthia Kennedy best. Whenever I visit Elinore I like talking to her. She's fourteen years old, large and woman shaped, and there's something about her—she always has a faraway look. I think that she could be pretty if she fixed herself up, but Aunt Sally says she can't, because the Kennedys are poor and they get all their clothes from yard sales.

Down the road less than a mile from the clearing there lives a creature so terrible that just the mention of his name, "Spook Wade," brings a chill of horror to any conversation. He's especially scary to kids who are always going into the woods and are afraid of running into him.

Everyone for miles around knows about Mrs. Mead's little five-year-old son, Bucky, who went into the woods to play ten years ago and never returned. A massive search was made for little Bucky Mead, but he was never found. Everyone says that Spook Wade got him. Except that Mrs. Mead says she doesn't believe it. Aunt Sally says she doesn't believe it, either.

I know everything there is to know about Spook Wade, and to me it's the best thing about the place where Elinore lives, although I'm a little apprehensive now that I know I'm going to stay there for so long. Still, Elinore has lived in the clearing for all of her life and she's never been dragged off. Whenever Elinore visits, we always talk about Spook, and I always say right before she leaves, "I hope this isn't the last time I see you, Elinore. I hope Spook doesn't just come out some night and climb into your window and get you."

Now, I'll be staying down the road from him, less than a mile, for a whole summer. The first thing Nelson says to me when I arrive is, "You better watch out Spook don't get you, Amanda. You're not in your nice, safe town anymore." Elinore smiles at me pleasantly, but all the kids are watching to see how I react.

I just smile like I'm interested but not afraid. I want to hear all about him, everything. In the back of my mind from the minute I hear I'm going to stay there is the idea that, somehow, I'll do what none of them have ever done—see Spook Wade and live to tell about it. If I can do that, it'll be the greatest triumph anyone has ever had. The important thing is to do it and not disappear like Bucky, of course.

Every day every kid who lives in the clearing comes out after breakfast and goes into the woods. The first few days I'm there it's mostly one long game of Pony Express, but on some days it's Robin Hood or Star Wars or a variation of Capture the Flag. It could be boring to go into the woods every day, but it never is because it's never the same.

Sometimes the Pony Express riders can't get through, and all the mail is captured. Or the army has to be called in to chase a gang who has stolen the mail because one of the bags contains gold. Sometimes there are aliens who become invisible.

One thing for sure, there's never a maiden in distress. If anyone would try to be one of those, she'd be sent home and never allowed to join in again. Even Cynthia Kennedy's little cousin, Marjorie Kent, who's only four years old, has to be an adult—an adult who doesn't do much, but still an adult.

Marjorie knows that. The second day I'm there someone runs smack into her and knocks her headfirst into a tree. She just staggers around and almost falls over, but she doesn't stop being an adult to be a crying little kid. She stands and rocks and holds her head for a few minutes like she's going to faint, while we all touch her and ask if she's all right, silently reminding ourselves to be more careful.

Marjorie says she's all right, and Cynthia's brother, Tom, takes her home.

When we get back we find that she has been taken to the hospital, and a piece of her skull is going to be sawed away to relieve the pressure on her brain.

The next day we hear that she's going to have a metal plate put over the place where her skull was. The skin will be sewn back over it with her hair still attached. Tom and his brother, Jarret, say they are going to call her "Marjorie Metal Head" when she comes home.

No one wants to admit that they were the ones who collided with her and bashed her into a tree, so everyone says Spook Wade did it. He was lurking behind the tree and suddenly stepped out and tried to kill her. But that isn't true. I saw who did it, and I know Nelson did, too. It was his sister, Annette.

✛ ✛ ✛

By the time I've been in the clearing for four days I'm so sick of Elinore telling me what to do I could just about throw up every time I hear her voice. Since I'm her guest, she expects to rule me like a third arm. "You can't go there, Amanda. Come here, Amanda. Don't do that, Amanda."

After I get really sick of it, I begin to notice that Elinore isn't just picking on me to boss around. She's kind of like a leader to all the kids who live in the clearing. She has a quick mind and a good imagination, and even our cousin, Nelson, who might be her equal, just isn't as fast a thinker. He's something like her lieutenant.

It's soon obvious to me that, if I don't get things rearranged in a hurry, it could get worse. In Stump I tell a whole army of kids what to do, but here, Nelson, seeing that Elinore expects me to do what she says, is also beginning to tell me what to do and expect me to do it. Things have to change, fast.

Nelson and I are coming down the logger's lane that runs through the woods. It's a hot, still afternoon, and we're the sole survivors of a massacred army supply train. I've hardly even had a chance to talk to Nelson alone before. It's lunchtime, and everyone else has gone to their separate houses for the eating and lying around that lasts through the heat of the afternoon until after supper.

After supper everyone comes out again. But at night no one goes into the woods. In the evening the games are just hide-and-seek or tag or Flying Dutchman, played in the clearing among the houses.

I say to Nelson, "Spook Wade didn't bump Margie into that tree. Annette did. You saw her."

Nelson immediately comes to his sister's defense. "Annette did not."

"Don't be silly. It was completely an accident, and anyway, I'd never tell. You ought to know me better than that." It's ridiculous that he'd even suspect me of tattling.

Nelson's a very mild-tempered boy, and he immediately says, "Oh, I know. It's just that, well, I told Annette I saw her slam into Marjorie, and she said she couldn't help it because Spook Wade pushed her from over behind the other tree where I couldn't see. You couldn't see him over there, either.

"Annette swears she saw this horrible, white, warty hand come out and it shoved her right into Marjorie. Annette's scared. She even had a nightmare about it last night. She thinks Spook wasn't trying to get Marjorie. He was trying to get her!"

What Nelson says worries me. I didn't see any hand, and Annette was running into the refuge so fast she didn't need a hand to push her. Still, maybe it's true. I don't know for sure, and there's no use talking to Annette. You can never get any sense out of her. She lies all the time, even when there's no reason. Still, even constant liars tell the truth every once in a while, and at the most inconvenient times. Like now, suppose this is one of her rare moments of truth, only I just assume she's telling one of her usual lies and then realize too late she isn't, when a horrible, white, warty hand comes out and grabs me.

But there is something else I really have to talk to Nelson about. That something is Elinore and how she always bosses me around. It suddenly comes to me how that could be changed. She tells Nelson what to do all the time. Maybe if

Nelson and I were together against her—Well, not really against, exactly, at least not so much that Elinore hates me. Can't have that since I'm staying with her. I even have to sleep in the same bed with her. Nelson and I will just have to stick together enough so that no matter what Elinore wants to do we decide to do something else and then get all the younger kids to go along with us. With all the younger kids with us, Elinore'll have to give in and go along if she doesn't want to be alone.

As soon as I tell him about it, Nelson agrees. "Yeah, she's so bossy. It's true, it's absolutely true. She bosses me around and tells me what to do all the time." Then he adds reluctantly, "Still, she can sure think of the good stuff . . ."

I interrupt, "Well, now's your chance. If we stick together on everything and do it right, she won't boss anyone anymore. Remember, Nelson, I'm only going to be here this summer, but if we get this right you can be free of her tyranny forever, even when I'm gone."

CHAPTER TWO

That night I'm especially sweet to Elinore so that she's lulled into a false sense of security. We're in bed and I pretend to go to sleep right away, although she wants to talk. I need quiet so I can plan.

Actually it's going to be easy. Every time Elinore suggests something to do, either Nelson or I come up with something different, then all the other kids'll go along with us.

The next morning Elinore is poking around dressing—she gets up slow and moves around slow in the morning. I gulp some cereal and skip across the clearing to Uncle Dan's house to make sure Nelson is still with me.

But when I say, "It's all worked out," Nelson looks blank.

"Elinore! We're going to challenge her today, remember?"

Nelson still looks blank, although there's a glimmer of light beginning to glow far off in the back of his brain.

I'm wildly impatient. Also distressed. Evidently it's not nearly as important to Nelson to shake off Elinore's tyranny as it is to me. Somewhere in his slow-moving brain he probably realizes that he's only going to exchange one girl cousin general for another.

"We have to do this together if it's going to work!" I get him alone and talk fast. "We have to be together!"

As the morning sun hits him, his enthusiasm gains, and he begins to make comments like, "Boy, won't Elinore be surprised when everything she wants to do, we decide to do something else!" He hesitates, then adds, "You'll have to be a really fast thinker though, Amanda, because old Elinore sure can come up with the good stuff."

"I am fast. Very fast. You've never had a chance to see that with Elinore always thinking things have to go her way. But at home there are always nine or ten kids who do what I say, some of them are even older than me. All of this stuff here is nothing compared to the things we do at home. You'll see."

Kids are moving toward us in the morning. Elinore says to me when she gets to us, "You went to sleep way before me, Amanda, that's why you got up so early." She looks irritable, as though she hasn't slept well. She also looks suspicious. Elinore can smell a rat a mile away.

We decide to play that three kids are caught in a bear trap up in the woods, and someone has been sent into the ranger station to get help in rescuing them. The three kids who are supposed to be in the trap—little ones who are always in some difficulty and have to groan and scream a lot and act like they need help all the time, run happily down the logger's trail to the place, way off, where they're supposed to be caught and where they're supposed to groan and scream until they're rescued.

Elinore decides she's going to be the one who rides into the station and in breathless tones describes the extent of their injuries—a lot of blood, and bones so badly broken they're sticking out through the skin, huge crunch marks from the trap. Then she begins organizing the rescue party. "Tom and Eunice will ride in and bring back the injured." An old wagon pulled with two ropes that are tied to each end of a broom handle will be the ambulance. "Jarret'll be the paramedic."

There are three escaped prisoners who have held up an armored car and who are to attack the rescue party as they bring in the injured. She'll be one of them. Nelson and I can be the other two. I nail Elinore with a determined look. "No, Elinore, Nelson and Jarret and I'll be the bad guys. You can be the paramedic."

She just looks at me. She can't believe I'm challenging her. Still holding her eyes I continue, talking to Jarret. "Jarret wants to be a bad guy, don't you, Jarret?" Jarret's surprised and bewildered. He looks from me to Elinore.

I smile sweetly at her. "You don't always have to decide things, do you, Elinore?"

She has been trying to be nice to Nelson and me by letting each of us be bad guys. But now that she knows I am going to keep up the challenge to her she's furious. The others see her fury and they're impressed. I'm even a little bit impressed. Elinore has a lot of force to her personality.

An argument begins about who should be what, and it goes on and on. Once we get a rescue party almost ready to leave, but Elinore changes who is what after I leave. Then I return and proclaim that an avalanche has fallen and buried Eunice, who has agreed with Elinore.

The kids who are supposed to be caught in the bear trap are tired of waiting and groaning, and they come straggling in to see what's holding everything up. Elinore tries to persuade them to go back, but as soon as she starts I scream, "They've been freed! They've been freed! Spook Wade freed them. But he's sent us this message!" My hand goes up to command complete silence. In my other hand there's an imaginary piece of paper:

"I've trained a killer bear,
And send to you this dare.
Come into my lair,
And we will eat you there."

There is a swell of appreciation from everyone, but when the poem is finished, I'm so awed with it myself and have taken so much energy thinking it up and making it rhyme that I've lost my momentum.

Elinore quickly fills the void with, "We never play Spook Wade here, Amanda. Never. That's too serious. He got Mrs. Mead's kid, Bucky. Spook Wade isn't a game here."

Everyone agrees with her instantly. Even Nelson, traitor Nelson, and my whole scheme collapses. Elinore promptly takes over and explains how it's going to be. There is triumph glinting in her eyes, and she is in complete control. She consolidates her position as supreme commander, and everyone falls into place. The glint of triumph becomes a full gloat.

Next, to punish me for even daring to challenge her she tells me I have to go along with the little kids who are caught in the bear trap and scream until I'm rescued. She says, "It won't take long now."

"I will not!" I exclaim. "I'm not going to be caught in a bear trap!" I square my shoulders and stalk off. Twenty feet away I turn and shout, "I'm going to commune with the forest. I'm going to find the force that makes all of you weak." At another twenty feet I turn to issue the ringing proclamation, "I'm going to look into the face of Spook Wade!" Then I turn and stride away with what I hope is impressive dignity.

But already there are tears spilling from my eyes. I've challenged Elinore and lost, and I have been completely beaten! There is still most of a summer left for me to stay in the clearing! I'll never get over this, never! Maybe I'll run away. I'll hitchhike all the way to Minneapolis where it's always winter. It certainly seems as bleak as winter to me. One thing for sure, they'll never see me cry.

When they can no longer see me, I run. I'm crying and running. There's no danger of getting lost; a little ridge runs through the whole woods, and to get out all you have to do is follow it to the road. I run up the logging road and beyond, to where the road turns into a trail, farther than I've ever gone. Far away. I'm going to run so far that I can sit and cry, maybe even scream. I'll scream and scream, and no one will be able to hear.

When I've gone so far I can't hear anything except the woods sounds and the sounds I'm making, I find a stump and sit down. Then I begin to wail. I grab handfuls of leaves to wipe my nose, then give myself up to crying. I cry out

my hatred of Elinore and Nelson. I wail out my homesickness for Stump, and I scream because Chad and Jessie have
gone away to Minneapolis, Minnesota, and left me alone.

After a long while, there is something. I become aware of
someone. Not close. There's no sudden chill of fear, like
Spook Wade is ten feet behind me or behind the next tree.
But there has been a sound or a movement while I was in the
middle of a great bundle of sobs. Something has alerted me.

Whoever it is, is still far away. I stop crying and am completely silent. I don't dare even move except to turn in a circle slowly, searching everywhere around me, even out into
the woods where the trees blend together. It's probably the
man who hauls logs out of the woods with his tractor. He
was way down the road and stopped to rest and heard this
dopey, crying kid. You can never really be alone anywhere.

In one of my turning, sweeping scans I find him. Very far
away, a thin, young man. So far away he's small. He's sitting
on a stump, motionless, and he's looking directly at me. It's
like he's observing a strange, interesting bird. He's definitely
not a logger.

The minute I actually see him, I'm gripped with fear. He
hasn't moved, but he can see that I see him. I jump to my feet
and begin to run. I run as fast as I can.

Every few seconds I throw a panicky look back over my
shoulder to see if he is following me. He isn't. When I have
gone a short distance I take a split second longer to look and
see that he is still sitting where he was, but he has turned
slightly and his eyes are following me.

I can't stop running, because a quick calculation tells me
that, even then, if he suddenly got up and began to run he

could still catch me long before I could reach Aunt Sally's house, or be anywhere near where the rest are.

I'm running as fast as I can when I reach the logger's road, and I'm looking back a lot, half expecting to see his lithe frame and long legs pumping toward me.

He didn't get me when he had the chance. He didn't even make a move once he heard me and saw me bawling to the trees. And in my brief glimpse of him he didn't seem threatening, maybe more like curious.

Far up ahead I see Cynthia Kennedy. I shout to her with my last breath. "Cynthia, Cynthia!" She glances around and then continues walking on slowly. My side is stabbing and I have to stop running. I skip for a while until I can begin again.

"Wait!" I shout. I have to shout it several more times before I can get enough breath to catch up with her.

As soon as I'm up with her, I begin to tell her about the man in the woods. But she doesn't seem interested. There are always kids around her in a high state of excitement. Tom and Jarret are her brothers, after all.

She has her usual faraway, worried look. But I go on, and after a while she looks at me with a mild level of interest and a touch of compassion. "You've been crying."

She's walking very slowly, but I still have to almost gasp to talk. "The man, he was sitting on a stump watching me! It was Spook! He could've killed me! You didn't see him, did you?"

Cynthia is losing interest, fast. She's always hearing "wild man in the woods" stories.

"There really was, Cynthia!" I make her look at me so I can be especially convincing. "There really was!"

She says mildly, "It's probably one of the loggers."

"No, I've seen the father and all of his sons. It isn't any of them. He's young, but not too young. Skinny, but not too skinny, and he's very pale. Do you know anyone like that?" Cynthia shakes her head.

"It's Spook Wade!" I shiver all over. "I told everybody I was going to find him, but I didn't think I really would. And now I did, and I've never been so scared in my life!"

Cynthia is looking at me, but she shakes her head again and looks away when I say it's Spook. "No, no one ever sees him. It had to be someone else."

It seems like there's something else she's going to say, but then she doesn't. And she's so certain it isn't Spook. It's almost like she knows who it is. I think of asking her. But then I don't.

We walk along in silence until I notice she's carrying a pen and a notebook. "Why do you have those?"

She has been looking like she's far away, but my question brings her back. "Oh, it's quiet in the woods, and I can read up there. I write poetry."

"Poetry!" I'm surprised. "Oh, I love poetry!"

She smiles at me. We're out of the woods and the sun is blazing hot.

"I have a lot of poems in my room," she says. "If you want to, you can come up and see them. Any of them you like I'll make copies for you."

CHAPTER THREE

I've never been in the Kennedys' house. It smells bad—old and like grease and kerosene. It's dingy and cluttered, and even before I go in the sounds of small children whining and complaining come out of the open windows.

On the way to the stairs we have to step over Cynthia's baby brother and sister. Her mother is working at the sink, and her creepy older brother, Lander, is sitting at the table staring into space.

Aunt Sally says people call the Kennedys "trash," but she says she'd never use that term for anyone. She says that they should be thought of as "unfortunate." She says their dad doesn't come home for weeks, and when he does sometimes he doesn't even bring home enough money for food. They don't have enough money to fix up their house, and they never go anywhere. She says it's only because

Mrs. Kennedy raises food in their garden that they have enough to eat.

Cynthia leads the way up dark, winding, narrow stairs. Then into a tiny room that is nearly filled by its only furniture, a small chest of drawers and a cot. The cot is neatly made and it's covered with a beautiful quilt that has many different patterns of pink fabric. The wallpaper is pink, too, but it's old and the only part of it that is visible has water stains. Not much of it is visible, because Cynthia's walls are almost all covered with poems that have been cut out of newspapers and magazines. There are poems thumbtacked everywhere.

Cynthia is watching me to see what I think of her room, and she looks pleased when I breathe, "Oh, I love this." She sits on the cot and opens one of the drawers.

"All the poems on the wall are my favorites. I'll copy any of them that you like, but you may just take one of these." She is gesturing to the drawer. Then she reaches under the cot and pulls out a box and adds, "Or one of these."

I'm enchanted. I begin to read the ones in the drawer, quickly and silently, and every now and then I say, "Oh, I like this," or, "Oh, this one!" In with the rest there are some that have "By Cynthia Kennedy" written at the end. One of them begins,

> Snow is falling,
> Swirling down
> Flakes of heaven
> Earth's white gown.

Trees with limbs
So brown and bare
Are laced with white
In snow filled air.

"This one makes me feel cold," I tell her. "It's hot in here, but I feel cold just from the words."

She smiles at me. "You're funny. You don't seem—how old are you, eleven?"

She thinks I'm mature. I'm thrilled, and also embarrassed.

"I don't know anyone else who likes poetry except me," she says. "Not a lot."

I smile back at her, "Well, I do."

From the wall to the drawer to the box I read, quickly and silently. Some of the poems are funny. I read from the wall,

A girl who weighed many an oz.
Used language I dared not pronoz.
For a fellow unkind
Pulled her chair out behind
Just to see (so he said) if she'd boz.

When she hears me laughing she looks up and asks, "Which one are you reading?"

I show her and she says, "There's another funny one on that wall."

I read,

This troubled world is sighing now;
The flu is at the door;
And many folks are dying now

Who never died before.

Down from it I see,

Little Willie from his mirror
Sucked the mercury all off,
Thinking, in his childish error,
It would cure his whooping cough.
At the funeral Willie's mother
Smartly said to Mrs. Brown:
"'Twas a chilly day for William
When the mercury went down."

She asks, "Did you ever read, 'The Cremation of Sam McGee' by Robert Service?"

"It sounds familiar. . . ."

"Up there." She points.

"Oh, yes, that one! I love that! Especially when he's sitting in the middle of the furnace, and he says,

'Please close that door.
It's warm in here
and I greatly fear
you'll let in the cold and storm.
Since I left Plumtree
down in Tennessee,
it's the first time I've been warm.'"

We both laugh.

Some of her poems are sad. Some are inspiring and beauti-

ful. All of the best ones are on her wall, and they all have perfect rhythm and rhyme.

She's leaning on her bed and writing in her notebook. It's
clear to me that she knows every poem on her wall.

Suddenly I think of a way that I can really impress her. "I
know a beautiful poem about a woman who has a horse that
she loves. It's called 'Kentucky Belle.' That's the horse's name.
Do you want to hear it? You'll love it."

She nods and I begin:

> "'Twas the summer of '63, sir,
> And Conrad had gone away,
> Gone to the country town, sir,
> To sell our first load of hay."

The stanzas flow into Cynthia's tiny room. They seem to
become a part of her little pink room. Cynthia is smiling.
There are tears in her eyes as she hears of the woman's love
for her homeland and her horse. We both feel the woman's
homesickness and fear. We feel her loss, and at the end we
are both inspired by her nobility.

There are tears in Cynthia's eyes and rapture on her face.
She smiles at me, and I feel that, at that moment, we are
somehow united by what we are sharing. The poem has been
a part of me and now I have given it to her. I have given her
something that I deeply love.

When it is finished there is a long time when neither of us
move or speak. We just sit in the hot summer morning.

But after a time, as though she is shaking free of a dream

she says, "Read this one. It's called 'The Collier's Dying Child.'"

I read:

> The cottage was a thatched one,
> It's outside old and mean.
> But all within the cottage,
> Was wondrous neat and clean.
>
> The night was dark and stormy,
> The wind was blowing wild.
> A patient mother sat beside,
> The deathbed of her child.

"This is the one I want."

"You can take it," she says. "I know the whole thing by heart. I'll make a new copy for myself."

I feel tremendously close to her. I lean back and begin to think about the morning.

Cynthia's reading, but then she reaches over to her drawer and pulls out an envelope. She opens it and takes out some papers. Handing them to me, she says, "Look at these."

They are shadowed pencil drawings, beautiful little pictures. A horse, a squirrel, lambs beside a barn, a little girl with a dog and a table with flowers.

"Oooh, they're beautiful," I tell her. "Did you do them?"

"No."

"Who did?"

She's reaching for them, and on her face there's a look like the one she had when we were coming down the logger's lane. It's like there's more she could say. "I found them."

The way she looks makes me feel funny, but I ask, "Where?"

I'm thinking that maybe she won't answer. Her expression is doubtful, but then she looks straight at me. "Can you keep a secret?" I nod.

"I'd like to tell you. You're just . . . a kid, but I like you. I need to tell someone."

I'm about to swear that I'd die rather than betray a secret when her eyes lock on me. "I'm going to tell you. But . . . Are you sure I can trust you? Are you sure you won't tell?"

I stare back at her, hard. "I'm sure. I won't tell."

She nods, and she's looking at the drawings so solemnly that I almost feel creepy. "When I'm up in the woods and I'm writing poems—sometimes it takes me a couple of days to get one just right—but when it's finished, when it's just right, I leave it there.

"The first time I just left it there by accident. I put it under a rock so it wouldn't blow away and forgot it."

There's something in the way she looks—"It's always gone the next day. Whatever I leave, it's not there when I go back. It's always a poem that I leave, but in its place, exactly where I left it, even though I put a rock on it to hold it, there's one of these instead. Whatever the poem's about, there's a picture about it when I go back the next day."

I reach out for the pictures and I'm almost afraid to touch them. A chill races through me and I try to make it stop by concentrating on a bee that is trapped by one wing in her window and is throwing itself over and over against the screen. "The man I saw up there," I tell her, "it could be him."

She breathes softly. "I don't know." We're studying each other intently. "Don't tell anyone," she repeats.

I nod. There's so much that I want to think about and so much I want to ask her, but I hear the kids coming back from the woods. I carefully fold my copy of "The Collier's Dying Child" and stand up to go. Before I turn to leave I say, almost formally, "Thank you, Cynthia. Thank you very much. Good-bye."

I know I have a lot of thinking to do. I'm going to have to think about the morning and about Cynthia and her pictures. I'll have to think for hours, maybe days. Just do nothing else but think.

But, there is something I have to think about right away, and that's the kids who are coming in from the woods. I have to face them.

The most important thing is that they not see I've been badly hurt. I have to look as though I've spent a wonderful morning and it hasn't mattered to me at all that Nelson betrayed me and Elinore crushed me. They can't ever suspect I've been crying.

I walk through the Kennedys' living room and watch them as they come. On my face there's carefully composed nonchalance. But as they get closer I suspect that maybe it isn't necessary. Maybe things didn't go so well while I was gone. For one thing, Elinore and Nelson aren't walking together. They are each walking alone. Elinore doesn't look like she's savoring any sort of victory. In fact, by the way they're walking—I begin to suspect that maybe it won't be too bad.

Usually all the kids are together laughing and kidding. But

not now. They all seem glum. Elinore's scowling, and Nelson's as far from her as he can be, and he's looking extremely stubborn.

I walk out onto the porch and call out gaily, "Hi, gang," as though I haven't seen that none of them are in a "Hi, gang," mood.

Nelson looks around at me like he thinks I've just come from another planet.

Elinore's scowl deepens until she remembers her earlier triumph. Then her face brightens and she comes out with, "Did you have a nice time alone?"

Before I can get out a nasty retort Nelson interrupts, "Shut up, Elinore." Then he turns to me, "Let's talk."

Now it's time for Elinore to look hurt, although she masquerades her feelings well and resurrects her scowl quickly.

I know that if I make even the smallest effort to act friendly, she'll fall all over herself being generous and try to reconcile with me, but I'm not going to give her an inch. I still remember how much gloating there was in the look she gave me just before I left.

CHAPTER FOUR

As soon as he says, "Let's talk," Nelson stalks off toward Mrs. Mead's porch. He doesn't even wait to see if I'm going to follow him.

On the porch I take one swing and he sits on the other. Mrs. Mead's porch is closed in by trellised climbing roses. Overhead there are grapes. As I sit down I think of little Bucky Mead and that he once lived here before he disappeared. He's been gone ten years—a little five-year-old kid who just vanished. I wonder if he spent all of his five summers playing here. I wonder if he was a sensitive little boy and if he noticed how beautiful it was. I wonder if he loved being here before he disappeared.

As soon as we sit down Nelson begins, "Gee, were you ever right about Elinore, Amanda! She's so bossy! She's such a bully!"

Hearing it from him is balm to my pained heart.

"I'm sorry I didn't stick with you. I'm just so used to doing everything her way. But after you left she was worse than ever—worse than anything. She wouldn't do anything I said, not even one little thing. Come with us tomorrow. Tomorrow'll be different, I promise. I'll never give in to her again!"

I look as though I have to think about it. Finally I say, "I might."

He responds, "I hope you do!"

We sit and swing. There are the sounds of bees and the smell of roses and grapes. I don't really believe that Nelson has changed and that he'll always stick with me against Elinore. But I do believe he intends to. Whether he does or not no longer matters, because now there is Cynthia and her poems and the man . . . Aunt Sally is calling us to lunch.

After we eat, I go out to the backyard and climb a tree. I need to be alone to think. Elinore brings her beautiful, expensive doll collection out onto the porch and sits arranging and posing them.

I'm up in the tree hanging from a limb by my knees so that my brain can get full of blood and I can think better. But my lunch is sitting on the bottom of my throat. After a while, I begin to swing back and forth until I'm flying out in a great arc. Then I straighten my legs and drop to the ground. It's a spectacular landing, just like a great gymnast. Elinore can't do that, so of course she says it's stupid. As soon as I land, I climb back up again.

Of all the things I have to think about, the most important is the man in the woods. Maybe I should go and tell Aunt

Sally about him, because he could be terribly dangerous. But Aunt Sally would ask a lot of questions, like why I wasn't with the others instead of off by myself in the first place, and Elinore would stick her nose into it and act like a jerk, and I don't want to go through any of that.

I begin to think of telling about Cynthia's poems and the pictures. But I've promised not to tell. I'm way up high in the tree now, high above the clearing. Actually, it's scary. One slip and I'd be dead, but being in a dangerous place helps you think about dangerous things.

After a while, I decide that I can't say anything to Aunt Sally about the man or Cynthia's poems and pictures. But I also decide I'll never go anywhere alone in the woods again, so I'll never have to worry about him. If he should appear when there are other kids around, one of us could surely be able to escape and run for help if he attacks us. So, that takes care of the man.

As for the poems and pictures, I've promised not to tell. And that's the difference between me and Nelson: I'm some-one who can keep a promise. Elinore, for instance, would love to know about the man and the pictures, but she'd go and tell her mother right away.

As soon as I realize that, I think maybe there's too much risk in not telling. Maybe I'm being very foolish not to tell. And maybe Cynthia is being incredibly stupid to go up there knowing someone has to be watching her.

From my place high up in the tree I can see Nelson com-ing out of his house and going back to Mrs. Mead's porch. I get down and go over. As soon as he sees me he says, "Boy, that Elinore! Who does she think she is, bossing us around the way she does! We'll show her! We'll . . ."

"Oh, Nelson," I interrupt. "I have something really important to worry about."

He looks surprised.

"It's a lot more important than Elinore and what she does. I'm worrying about something that could be dangerous."

He gives me a sharp look. I can tell he doesn't believe me. I'm sitting, thinking.

He expects me to go on, but when I don't he fidgets. After a few seconds he says, impatiently, "What?"

"I can't tell you."

He's just looking at me. "Why not?"

"Like I said, it could be dangerous, and it's something I promised not to tell."

He's beginning to frown, though he still looks doubtful. "Who?"

"Who what?"

"Who'd you promise not to tell?"

"I can't even tell that."

He's getting really irritated. "You don't have a secret. You're just making something up."

"Oh, yeah?"

"Yeah."

"Well, I do have a secret, and I'd like to talk about it. But . . ." I'm quiet again, and it's really getting on his nerves.

"Even if you just made something up, you could tell me."

I'm actually considering telling him. I'm at least thinking of getting close to the subject. Maybe saying, What if, and then describing something like, what if there was a man in the woods who gave this girl pictures and stuff? Then I could get his opinion without really telling him anything.

"I'd like to talk about it," I tell him. "It's so scary. I wish I could tell you, and then you could tell me what you think. . . ."

He has been ignoring me, but he turns around and gives me a penetrating look. I can tell he's beginning to suspect there might actually be something. He's still not drooling with curiosity, but he starts to pelt me with questions.

I don't answer. "I made a promise, and when I give a promise I don't ever break it. Promises mean something to me. I can't trust you."

He looks at me, hurt. But then he declares, "Yes you can! Just because I didn't stick with you this morning, it doesn't mean anything. My dad's a preacher, and I know a lot of things I'd never tell anybody. If something's important, I don't tell."

He's insulted, and he doesn't care about the secret anymore. He just cares about his honor.

"I believe you," I say, and the odd thing is, I really do.

Over in the Kennedys' yard Cynthia is hanging out wash. Suddenly a mental picture comes to me of her sitting alone in the woods with a man creeping up close to watch her. He's watching, and then when she leaves he comes and gets her poem and reads it. Then he sits down and draws. I know I'm just going to have to talk to someone.

"Stay here," I say to Nelson. "Wait until I come back. I have to talk to Cynthia."

Cynthia is holding a wet sheet, and when she sees me she gestures to it. "Can you grab that?" I take hold of one end of the sheet and pin it to the line while she pins the other. Then she reaches down into the wicker wash basket for something else to hang.

While she's still stooped over and not looking at me I say to her, "I'd like to tell someone."

She straightens up and looks at me, kind of shocked. She's fastening a man's undershirt to the line, and I'm watching her face. I can see that she doesn't like the idea. She doesn't look at me for a bit, but when she finally does, she asks, "Why? Who are you thinking of telling?"

Still studying her face closely to get her reaction I say, "Nelson."

"Nelson!" There is complete surprise. "Why him?"

I'm not sure myself at first, so I don't answer. But after a minute I begin, "Someone should know and he . . ."

"Well, I don't want a lot of people knowing. He'd tell."

I don't know how to explain it. "That's the thing, I don't think he would." I hesitate a little and then go on. "I'd make him promise to God."

She's finished with the wash. She picks up the basket and stands swinging it back and forth in front of her. Finally, she says, "Oh, I don't know. Maybe. Okay, I guess."

Back on Mrs. Mead's porch Nelson is capturing ants. "I can tell you," I say to him, "but you've got to promise to God never to tell anyone else."

He continues capturing and releasing ants, and he doesn't answer. He isn't even looking at me.

"I can't tell you if you don't promise." He looks up for a second and then down quickly. The biggest ant is crawling up the leg of his shorts and he has to divert it.

"I promise."

"To God. Promise to God, not to me."

"I promise to God."

"Okay, now remember, only you and me and Cynthia can know this." Four ants are trying to escape and his hands are flying around as he tries to keep them from getting away.

"This morning after you betrayed me . . ." He winces. "I went way deep into the woods."

He's adding three more big, black ants, and they're all over his arms and legs. Swiftly, trying not to crush them, he's directing them all over himself.

"Well, I found Spook!" There's no response. I know he thinks I'm making it up. "At least I think I did. There was a tall skinny man. I was sitting on a stump and he came toward me."

Nelson glances up quickly. He thinks I'm suddenly starting to believe made-up stuff. "It was a logger," he declares.

"No, it wasn't. I've seen them and it wasn't them."

He gives me a sharp look.

"I ran when I saw him. I ran down the logging road. Cynthia Kennedy was way down in front of me. I told her about it, and she said it was a logger, too. But, Nelson, it wasn't. It was someone else."

He doesn't want to believe me. "It could've been anyone." If he believes me he has to stop directing ants and really think about what I'm saying.

I stare at him. When I'm sure he isn't going to contradict me anymore I go on. "There's more. Cynthia says she goes up the logger's road all the time. She sits up there and writes poems. Then she leaves them there. And the next day when she goes back her poem is gone, and there's a picture there instead. Someone takes her poem, and makes a picture and leaves it there for her."

Finally, I have all of his attention. There are ants crawling everywhere, but I still have his attention because he's just brushing them away. "That's weird!" he exclaims. "And it could be dangerous!"

"Yeah," I breathe. We're both quiet, thinking.

Then I ask, "And who is it?" Just saying it makes me shiver.

"You think the guy you saw is the same one who's giving her the pictures?" Nelson asks.

"Yeah," I answer. "And it's Spook. I just know it."

Nelson shakes his head. "It can't be."

"Why not? If it isn't Spook, who is it?"

He's still shaking his head. "No one ever sees Spook. He's something . . . something like autos . . . It wouldn't be him."

"Autos?"

"Yeah. Dad told me about it. He doesn't talk. He just sits and rocks or something."

I'm not convinced, but I try other possibilities. "Maybe it's some guy who's in love with Cynthia. But wouldn't some guy who's in love with her just walk up to her and say, Hi, Babe, or, Hi, Beautiful Maiden, or something like that?" We both giggle.

Nelson has begun capturing ants again, but it's just something to keep his hands busy while he thinks. I'm already beginning to wonder why I chose him to tell, of all the people I could have chosen. "What'll we do?"

"Do?" Nelson looks up at me and I can see another half hour of ant-corralling and silent thought coming.

So I say to him, "I'll come up with a plan."

Actually it doesn't take long. "Let's follow Cynthia up there when she goes. We could hide under some bushes and watch for him. He'll be watching her, and when she leaves we can follow him back to where he lives and find out who he is. Or, maybe we should go up early in the morning. Cynthia'll have to know so we know where to wait. We'll have to hide and be quiet and not move and wait all day."

Nelson's face is furrowed in thought. He considers, but then shakes his head. "Some things are just too dangerous, Amanda. Remember Bucky." He's whispering because we're on Mrs. Mead's porch.

I shudder, and then I begin to weigh all that I've heard about Spook Wade against this new image of a man who leaves drawings in exchange for poems. I think about the slender man I glimpsed as he sat watching me.

Aunt Sally and Elinore are calling. It's time to go in.

"Wash your hands in the laundry room," Aunt Sally says. "I don't want you near this hot fat." She's deep-fat frying scrapple, and it takes all of her attention.

I slide in behind the table after my hands are washed. It's a good time to ask her about Spook because she can't get away, and there are things I have to know now. "Aunt Sally, what is Spook?" If I can get it out of her without Elinore butting in, then maybe I'll know the right thing to do.

Aunt Sally glances up for an instant and then back down to the pan. "This is tricky, Amanda. What's that again?"

"She wants to know about Spook," Elinore pipes in.

"There's nothing about him to tell," Aunt Sally answers.

"Is he a real person?"

She looks at me as though I'm being ridiculous. "Of course he's real. His mother was my sixth grade teacher. Heavens, what a strange woman she was! He's her only child. A lot of people think he's strange because of her, that she just pressured him and kept at him, pushed and pushed him and was never satisfied, so he just retreated into himself. She was—is—really odd."

"Nelson says Spook is autos. What's that?"

"It means he's a car." From Elinore. She's laughing and grabbing her stomach.

"It means autistic. That's what the psychiatrists said he was when he was little. But Dolly Mead says she never believed that he was."

"What's it mean, being autistic?"

"It's a condition where people who have it don't respond normally."

"So, when he went to school he was in special ed or something?"

Aunt Sally looks surprised. "No, oh no. He didn't go to school. He never got that far. He just sat and rocked. That's what I've heard."

"Why?"

"Why what?"

"Why did he just sit and rock?"

From Elinore, "Because he's weird."

I have to repeat everything to get past her. "Why did he just sit and rock, Aunt Sally?"

"What, dear? Ouch! I always burn myself when I fry scrapple this way, but it's so good when it's done right."

"Why did he just sit and rock?"

"Well, that's the thing. No one knows. People who are autistic do that, so that's why they thought he was autistic."

"They just sit and rock?"

"Yes. No one knows why, although I guess scientists are investigating it and trying to figure it out. But people who are autistic, I believe, are that way from early childhood. From what I've heard he was perfectly normal until he was about four. That's what Dolly Mead says."

"So, he didn't have to go to school because he sat and rocked?"

"She thinks she's going to sit and rock and she won't have to go to school," Elinore says.

"They don't just let you stay home because you want to," Aunt Sally says. "He was evaluated a lot. His mother quit teaching and tried to work with him. He has always just been there with her. Except when he was older, up around fourteen or so. Then he started coming out at night, and people would see him.

"I guess he was sneaking out after she went to sleep. Anyway, he'd peep in people's windows. Several different times people woke up and he was standing right beside their beds in the moonlight. It was mostly moonlit nights that he came out. Naturally that got him in trouble with the police."

"So now his mother chains him to his bed," Elinore says in a ghoulish voice. "But he picks the lock and comes out at night and eats people."

"Elinore!" Aunt Sally warns.

"Scoops their brains out with a spoon."

"That'll be enough!" Aunt Sally's eyes are flashing. Elinore goes blank.

"When he started going into people's homes, the police said he'd have to be put in a juvenile detention center, but his mother said she'd see that he never got out to do that again. I don't know . . . You don't know why people do the things they do. It's hard to tell why they are the way they are. He was always very shy; when he was in day care, people said he was so shy he hid when anyone looked at him. He'd go back in under a desk.

"He didn't ever talk much, and eventually he didn't talk at all. Finally he was just hiding under the desk all the time. He stayed there except to go to the bathroom. And then he stopped coming out even to go to the bathroom, just did it there. That's when his mother stopped teaching and stayed at home with him.

I guess no one could figure out what to do for him, so eventually they gave up trying to reach him or communicate with him.

"Do you think he killed Bucky Mead?"

Aunt Sally glances up at me. "No one knows. Bucky disappeared around the time when he was being seen out a lot. I remember his mother being so . . . tense, and now she's what you would call a recluse."

"That's a lady hermit," Elinore says.

"Something like that," Aunt Sally says. "No one ever sees her. Her husband died, and it's just her and the son there. . . . Well, he's a man, now. You know Dolly Mead's her sister . . ."

"What!" From me.

Elinore smirks. "Yeah, Mrs. Mead's Spook's auntie. There's a lot you don't know about down here."

Aunt Sally says patiently, "Well, how could she, dear?" Then she goes on. "Dolly talks to her sister every day, but since she's a recluse no one can really get close to her."

Aunt Sally rushes to the sink with the pan. "I knew if you got me talking, I'd ruin this!"

"So, Spook's just some guy who's like, retarded?"

"What? Oh no, I don't think so. Not retarded. I don't know what he is. I don't think anyone does.

"Well, this is definitely ruined! You know I can't talk and cook at the same time!"

"When Bucky disappeared didn't the police come and try to find out if he did it?"

Aunt Sally is throwing all the scrapple away. After she plops it in the garbage bucket, she looks around at me. "Oh, they investigated. But his mother told them he no longer even left his room, that he was completely incompetent. And when they tried to talk to him, well, I imagine he didn't give them much satisfaction. There wasn't much they could do. Nothing ever came of the investigation."

CHAPTER FIVE

There's a lot I have to think about, but Elinore wants to talk and talk about taking gymnastics and swimming. "Can you float on your back?" she asks.

"No. Yes. Some. Can you?"

"Of course. Except in the ocean. I can't even swim in the ocean."

"I love the ocean."

"I do, too," Elinore says, "especially the Pirate Ship. But I also love the Whirl Around and the Werewolf's Cave."

I just look at her. "Pirate Ship? Werewolf's Cave? What's that? It sounds like the fair."

She's looking at me like I'm being ridiculous. "The board-walk, silly. Haven't you ever been to the ocean? Haven't you ever jet skied? Or played miniature golf or . . . ?"

"I've been to the ocean lots of times, but there's none of that stuff. It's just rocks and gulls, or . . ."

"Rocks! Not even sand!" She seems completely shocked.

"Well, some sand, but mostly rocks."

"What kind of dumb ocean do you go to?"

"Maine. Or Nantucket. On Nantucket there are these houses with big, puffy, blue flowers. It's so great."

"Rocks! And no boardwalk?"

"No."

"That's dumb."

I just turn my back to her. I have to think about other things, like Cynthia. And why she told me, of all people, about the pictures.

After I think about it for a while I decide that it's probably because she has no one else. I never see her out walking with any girlfriends or giggling with a boyfriend. There isn't anyone around who's her age who lives in the clearing. So she talks to me even though I'm younger than she is.

All I ever see her doing is working. She has so many little brothers and sisters, and maybe she's embarrassed about living in a house that isn't fixed up.

Anyway, she can come up with fun stuff. Like she had this costume contest where all the girls, Elinore and Annette and Eunice and I, had to be fancy ladies, and all the boys had to be either pirates or clowns or dogs. Nelson was a chow. He put a wig on his face and a fuzzy rug on his body. Jarret was a clown. Tom was a pirate.

Usually girls her age just talk about boys all the time, but maybe all the girls her age think she's weird because she's always reading poetry. After I think about her for a while I decide that, if she doesn't have any other friends maybe I'm the only one she has to talk to.

Anyway, I like her, and she needs us. I think about how I'd feel if she were to go up to the woods and disappear forever. Or, what if she went up there and they found her murdered. Then I'd have known about her pictures and poems and stuff and not have done anything about it. I'd be horrified because I hadn't told anyone.

After I think about that for a while, I feel pretty sure someone has to stop her from going there ever again before it's too late.

Several times I almost tell Aunt Sally everything, the man and the poems and drawings. But I've promised. I've made a solemn promise, and I've even made Nelson promise to God, which is just like if I had promised to God. After I think about it some more, I decide that I can't, I really won't say anything.

But, all the time I'm wondering why Cynthia doesn't have sense enough, herself, to be afraid. Doesn't she realize it's dangerous? I mean, sitting in the woods with a stranger creeping around! Before I go to sleep I decide to go to Cynthia the first thing the next morning and talk to her about why she should be afraid.

Elinore tries to make up with me several times. She's seen Nelson and me together, and I can tell she's pretty upset. She acts almost tame. I should be delighted, but the new stuff about Cynthia takes up so much space in my brain that I don't have any space left for Elinore.

The next morning is rich and beautiful, a morning that

heaven should be like if you have to spend eternity there. All the kids are coming out, and Elinore says to me, "You can decide stuff today. We'll take turns. You do it one day, and I'll do it the next."

I'm suspicious, and I'm thinking when Jarret says, "I painted Lander's old bike."

He's looking at me like I should care. "For the circus we're having, remember?"

"Oh, yeah."

"It's over in the shed." He goes to the shed and brings it out. It's a real old bike and it's painted with hot pink stripes and purple and green spots. We're all admiring it.

"I'm going to stand on the handlebars while he rides it," Tom says. "I'm the acrobat. The only thing is, it doesn't have any brakes."

I look at it and then say, "It's not supposed to. It's an old-fashioned bike. They didn't have brakes you squeeze with your hands. You had to pedal backward."

"Pedal backward?" Jarret looks like I'm making it up.

"Yeah, you just pedal backward, and then it stops. Try it, you'll see."

He gets on and starts down a steep slope toward a ditch. At first he's just coasting, but then he starts pedaling really fast. "Okay, now, pedal backward," I yell. But he doesn't. He's just like, frozen.

I'm shouting, "Pedal backward!" Everyone else starts to shout, "Pedal backward! Then we all go, "Ohhhhh!" as the bike hits the ditch and flips over, with Jarret landing on his head.

I'm horrified, and I'm thinking he's probably dead, or at

least paralyzed for life, but then he gets up and calls to us, kind of like, ordinary, "I forgot to remember."

Everybody's laughing when Nelson arrives. He looks grumpy, and I wonder if he has been up half the night thinking about Cynthia and everything instead of sleeping. If he has been, then maybe it wasn't such a mistake to choose him to tell. I haven't lost any sleep over it, and I'm relaxed and filled with energy.

Right away Nelson says, "Amanda, I want to talk to you." As soon as Elinore hears that, she knows we're into something together that she isn't going to be a part of, and she's absolutely furious.

"You two are so rotten," she says. She's almost sputtering. "You are rotten, dopey lovers! Go off by yourselves, you dopey lovers! You can't be with us!"

I shoot Elinore a disgusted look, and Nelson says, almost absentmindedly, "Shut up, Elinore. Go play."

She looks as though she's ready to explode. "Come on," she says to the younger kids, "let the dopey lovers alone."

But the younger kids sense that Nelson and I are into something and they hesitate, looking from Nelson to me.

"Go with Elinore," Nelson says to them, and after they hang around for a few more minutes they reluctantly straggle away with her.

Elinore tries to get Tom and Jarret and some other kids to chant, "Lovers, lovers, see the dopey lovers," as they leave, but she can't get them to keep it up for very long.

As soon as we're alone, Nelson says in a decisive tone, "I've been thinking, Amanda, you and Cynthia can't go up to the woods with this guy around. It's too dangerous. I'll go." He's striding purposefully toward the Kennedys' house while he's talking, and I have to almost skip to keep up with him. "I'll go and leave him a note."

Listening to him I can hardly believe he's the same old Nelson. What a difference a night of thinking makes! He's never talked this much and now he's positively taking charge. I wonder if the change is permanent.

Cynthia is sweeping the back porch when we get there, and she smiles when she sees us. Nelson says, "Come with us." He doesn't stop to see if she's coming, he just continues on toward the bench under the apple tree.

Cynthia looks questioningly at me, and I roll my eyes. I hope she doesn't think he's an idiot because of the way he's acting.

When we're seated on the bench under the tree he says, "That guy who gives you pictures could be Spook. I don't think it is, but it could be." He's looking hard at Cynthia as though he intends to make her believe it if she decides to argue.

She just nods.

"He could be crazy sometimes and not sometimes. He could draw pictures for you ten times and then murder you." Nelson sounds very forceful. "You can't go there anymore."

Cynthia looks at him, surprised and as though she's going to say something but then thinks more about it and decides not to.

"Now, here's what we'll do," Nelson says. "I'll take him a letter. I'll go up there with it and you two can wait down where the loggers are. I'll whistle if I'm in trouble. If you hear me whistle, tell the loggers and get them to come and get me.

I'll leave a trail if I'm captured, the usual things." Nelson looks desperate and tragic and excited all at once. "If you don't hear a whistle but I'm still not back in half an hour, go get the loggers."

Cynthia looks impressed. "Nelson, that's so noble! You sound . . . so grown-up, so much like you're not a kid."

I'm just looking from her to him. I half expect Nelson to pretend to throw up. Or maybe stand up and beat his fists on his chest and give the Tarzan call. But he just acts like, of course she thinks that, because it's true.

"And you're probably right," Cynthia says. "I've been thinking about the man who leaves the drawings, that he might be Spook." She's looking off to the line where the trees begin.

I'm deeply shocked, and I wonder how she could ever go up there if she thought that! She has actually gone up there several times!

As if to answer she says, "I know Spook's supposed to have killed Bucky, but the person who leaves the drawings . . . I don't know . . . I'm not afraid of him. After the first drawing I was, a little, but I'm not now."

"Bucky . . ." Nelson begins.

Cynthia draws in a deep breath. "I . . . There's something . . ."

Suddenly, I don't know why, but I don't want her to go on. It's the way she looks. Nelson doesn't seem to notice. He's just gazing at her steadily.

She looks upset. "Maybe it's time I talked to someone. You kids . . ." I glance at Nelson, but I can't catch his eye. She's going on. "I think . . . I never told anyone . . ."

I feel like saying to Nelson, She's going to tell us something. I want to say, Can't you see it? Can't you tell? But he won't look at me.

Cynthia is shaking. She says, "I don't think Spook did anything to Bucky."

It seems like Nelson is holding his breath, and he asks, "Do you know who did?"

She's looking directly at him. "I'm going to tell you something, Nelson, you and Amanda. I have to tell someone, and for some reason, even though you are both kids, I trust you." She looks terrible.

Nelson's nodding. I want to scream at him, We can't hear this.

"Lander," she begins, "my brother, I think he—not on purpose, it was an accident . . ." Nelson is sucking in his breath and he finally glances at me. I'm shaking my head at him, but he just looks away. It's too late to say anything.

"Lander was just a kid when Bucky disappeared. I was four, Margie's age. I remember Bucky, and I remember that day. Everyone was talking about it, and everyone was hunting him.

"Bucky and I used to play together. We raced our big wheels. He said we were going to get married. It's funny, I can't remember his face, although sometimes I think I can. Sometimes I think I can still see his eyes staring at me."

Nelson is looking at his hands, as though he no longer can look at her.

She goes on, "I don't know for sure, but I think I know where he is." Her eyes are upon us briefly, but then she's looking up to the sky.

"Lander says things when he drinks. He gets drunk and he says . . . It's stuff about a kid who's locked in a refrigerator."

"A refrigerator!" Nelson and I both exclaim.

"On a dump!" she adds softly.

In unison we echo, "A dump!"

Cynthia's face is splotched red and very white, and her voice is quavering. Nelson's eyes are riveted upon her.

Her voice is almost a whisper. "I think Lander killed Bucky!" Tears are streaming down her face.

From Nelson there comes a low whistle.

"Bucky died, I think . . . in a refrigerator!" Her face is in her hands and she's sobbing. "I shouldn't be telling you this," she sobs. "It's something I can't even stand to think about!"

"Yeah," I breathe out softly.

But Nelson says, "You can talk to us."

She stands up and she's searching in her pocket for a hand-kerchief, then she begins walking, automatically, as though she's sleepwalking. Nelson and I are with her, one on either side. We're going toward the logger's road. All around us there is heavy summer and the smell of honeysuckle, the sounds of bees.

I'm thinking, if Chad and Jessie hadn't gone away to stupid old Minneapolis and left me here, then I wouldn't be hearing any of this. I'd be at home in Stump, talking to my friends or riding my bike. Awful things don't happen in Stump, or if they do I never hear about them.

Cynthia seems to be almost talking to herself, except that Nelson and I are with her. "Lander's seven years older than me. But when I was nine—he was sixteen—I showed him some of my poems. And he said they were stupid.

"I said, 'Bet you can't write a poem this good.'

"He went and got one that he had written and showed it to me. It was about a little kid who was locked in a refrigerator . . . and died." Nelson and I lean out to see the horror on each other's faces. Cynthia adds in a whisper so soft we can barely hear it, "With a snake."

"A snake!"

She stops walking and rubs her face with her hands, then slowly her faraway look comes and she goes on.

"The end of the poem had a tree growing beside the dump. And a storm came up, with lightning and thunder. The lightning hit the tree and made it fall on the refrigerator! The refrigerator was crushed, and the little boy inside it was crushed! Everything was crushed!"

I want to scream, "I knew I didn't want to hear this!" But I can't.

Nelson is the first one to say something. It sounds desperately hopeful. "Oh, Lander probably made it up." I can tell he's really trying to think of some way she could be wrong. "He probably just imagined how Bucky could have died and then made up this story poem about it. It sounds good. Boy, that Lander's got a good imagination."

Cynthia shakes her head. "I thought of that, too. I didn't want to believe it. But when Lander's drunk he says things, he talks about it. It's a lot more now. I never said anything to anyone about it before, but he talks about it a lot now. I don't know . . . I wish I knew what to do."

"What does he say, exactly?" Nelson asks.

"Oh, like, 'I didn't mean it.'" She's shaking her head.

She and I sit down on a log, and Nelson is opposite us,

mechanically stepping on and off a stump. "Why would Lander do anything like that to Bucky?" he asks. "I mean, what did he have against a little kid like that? Ten years ago. What, was Bucky a really rotten little brat?"

Cynthia looks up into the trees, and it seems almost as though she has gone away from us and is up there, as though she has escaped the earth. But then she comes back. "No, he wasn't horrible. He took my truck and dropped it down the window well, but he was just a normal kid.

"Lander says Bucky was calling him names, and he only put him in there to scare him. He didn't mean to leave. He was just going to stand off to one side and wait until Bucky really began to cry before he let him out. But all of a sudden it started lightning and raining really bad. It was raining so hard it was like walls of rain. And then the big tree fell. It fell right on Lander, and he was caught in its branches. He almost couldn't get loose.

"The lightning made his hair burn. He was so scared he just ran and ran until he got back home. And after he was home he was afraid to say anything. When they were hunting for Bucky they asked him if he'd seen him, and he just shook his head.

"I don't remember the storm or Lander coming home, but I remember everyone crying. And the police. They thought my big wheel was his and they were going to take it.

"Lander says he never went back up there until a year ago, and by then there was nothing anyone could see. The refrigerator was completely covered by the tree. That big, old rotten tree covered everything." Cynthia is sitting with her head in her hands.

I'm thinking, it couldn't have been like that. A kid couldn't have just gone out one morning to play and then died with no one ever knowing what happened. Except that I know it did. I know Cynthia's horrible, disgusting brother did it.

I'm not going to be able to think about it for very long. I'll just have to think about it for a few seconds and then maybe I'll wait until my brain gets calm before I have to think about it again.

After a short while Nelson says, "Me and Amanda gotta go now, Cynthia."

Cynthia gets up and starts walking slowly back down toward the clearing, but Nelson and I aren't with her. She doesn't seem to notice what we're doing.

When she's pretty far away I come out with, "Hey, Nelson!"

He doesn't say anything. We're walking together, but it's like we're alone. Until we hear the other kids. Then we begin sneaking along, dodging from tree to tree. As soon as we're near enough, we spring out and wreck their whole convoy.

Elinore is furious. "They were army trucks, you idiots! They were full of medical supplies for a field hospital! Can't you see the red crosses on the sides?"

We look. It's just juice from some poisonous red berries. You'd have to know it's there to see it.

Later, when we're walking back, Elinore says to Nelson, "Amanda hasn't ever even been to the beach."

"I have," Nelson says.

"I have too," I declare. "Just because it wasn't the same . . ."

"She was to a beach that had rocks instead of sand."

"I liked the beach," Nelson says. "I liked the horses."

"Horses!" From both Elinore and me.

He looks from me to her, like, what?

"You're both nuts," Elinore says. "You're making stuff up. There aren't horses at the beach, and there's always sand."

"There were too horses," Nelson declares.

"I don't remember you ever going to the beach." Elinore looks at him suspiciously. "When were you at the beach?"

Nelson is looking ahead, and he seems reluctant to answer, but then he says, "When I was five."

"Oh, after your mother died," Elinore says.

He doesn't reply.

CHAPTER SIX

Nelson and I don't have a chance to be alone to talk to each other because we're busy planning the circus, but in the middle of the afternoon we both go to Mrs. Mead's porch again. I hope that no one thinks we're weird because we're together so much, but I have to talk to him.

Mrs. Mead's porch has so many grapevines and roses that it seems like a private little flower house. The first thing I notice when I step into it is that Nelson isn't penning ants. He's just sitting on the swing, perfectly still, staring into space.

I plop down onto the swing beside him and push my feet to make the swing move. Then I say the word, "Lander!" The name just hangs in front of us like a spider that has come down one long thread.

"Why didn't anyone think of him doing it before?" I ask.

"Didn't they think he might have? I mean, didn't he change or something after that, and wouldn't someone figure it out?"

Nelson gets up and goes to sit on the porch rail. He wiggles backward until he's completely hidden by the grapevines. When he speaks there's only his voice coming out of the vines, and it seems like the vines are talking. "Everyone was so certain it was Spook."

"So they didn't even think of Lander?"

"I guess not. Lander was only, what did Cynthia say, eleven?"

"I can't understand it. How could he just go on?"

From the grapevine, "What else would he do? He couldn't just decide to tell and then tell. You know what would happen to him."

"Yeah." I kick the swing to make it go faster.

"And the Kennedys," from the grapevine, "they're . . . you know."

"Unfortunate?"

"Yeah. And their dad . . ."

I'm quick with, "Cynthia's okay."

Nelson agrees, "Yeah, but she's like she's not really a part of them. Their dad. . . . They don't have enough money. The church gives them stuff and like that. And Lander doesn't hardly work."

"Where does he work?"

"Body work."

"What? He digs up bodies!"

A huge laugh explodes from the grapevine. "No, auto bodies. Body and fender. He fixes wrecked cars."

"Oh." A while goes by, and then the grapevine whistles in

a low exclamation, "And all this time everyone thought it was Spook!"

We're silent some more, but thoughts are weaving between us.

"Maybe Spook did do it and Cynthia's wrong?" Even as I say it I don't think it's possible.

"No, that stuff about the lightning and the refrigerator . . . and the snake, especially the snake . . ." Nelson's voice is low and filled with dread. "It happened!"

Suddenly I'm angry. "I don't like awful stuff! Cynthia shouldn't have told us. Now we're going to have to tell somebody."

Nelson pokes his head out. "Why?"

"Because . . . It's so awful! And that man who leaves the pictures . . . ?"

Nelson looks at me like he thinks I'm coming unglued. "It's Cynthia's problem." He's trying to sound soothing. "And Lander's . . ."

"Yeah." I'm swinging for a while, and then I say to him, "Cynthia taught me how to read minds."

He looks out at me. "That's impossible."

"No, it isn't. The first day I got here she was weeding the flowers, and I was talking to her and she taught me. Want to see?"

He's just staring.

"Let's go talk to her. You'll see."

We go over to the Kennedy house, and a man's voice calls out when we knock on the screen door. "Come in." Lander's at the kitchen table. He has an apple and a long knife. He cuts a piece off the apple and then brings the knife up to his mouth. His beard is stubbly and his eyes are red. It seems like he has a hard time focusing, but when his eyes settle on me I feel like running.

Behind me I hear Nelson suck in his breath. It's so loud I'm afraid Lander'll hear. My voice as I ask, "Cynthia in?" is supposed to sound light and airy, but when it comes out it sounds quivery. Lander gestures toward the stairs with the knife, and Nelson and I hurry past him.

I'm more afraid of Lander now than I ever was of Spook. Spook never seemed real because we never saw him. But Lander's real and he's always there. He's there every day.

Cynthia is just sitting up. Our stomping up the stairs has awakened her, and there are little triangular shapes from her quilt still pressed onto her face where she's been sleeping. She looks sweaty and distant, but when she sees us she says, "Oh, hi. I fell asleep. I was awake till three o'clock last night, reading."

With her, Nelson and me in her tiny room there's almost no square foot of space left. Nelson turns her empty waste can over for a seat, and I hunch on the end of the cot opposite her. He's looking around amazed at all the poems.

I start right in with, "Nelson doesn't believe we can read each other's minds. Let's show him."

"Nobody can read anybody else's mind," he declares. "That's dumb."

Cynthia doesn't really even look at him, but she says, "Amanda and I can exchange thoughts through the air without words." She says it with a mysterious look, and her voice is very low and strange, as though she's a weird magician.

Nelson frowns at her.

Cynthia hands him a piece of paper. "Here, because you are

a gentleman and a scholar we'll show you. Write a word on this, a short one. We have just begun to develop our psychic skills so we can't do long messages. But write one word, a three letter one, and I'll transmit it to Amanda. Be sure not to let her see it."

To me she says, "Turn your back, Amanda."

Nelson is still frowning but he wraps himself around his paper so I can't possibly see and begins to write. Even if I tried to sneak a peek I couldn't. When he's finished writing he folds his paper over and over and hands it to Cynthia. He watches me all the time to make sure I'm not able, somehow, to see.

Cynthia opens it and silently reads it, then she carefully folds it again. "Please be very quiet," she says to him. "It takes a lot of energy to transmit even one word. And Amanda must concentrate really hard to receive it.

"This is so difficult," she says. "I'll have to go into a trance." She closes her eyes and starts swaying as though she's concentrating very hard. After a while she opens her eyes and looks at me. "Do you know what the word is?"

I shake my head, and she says, "I'll have to snap my fingers to clear the air. It must be cluttered with outside thoughts." She snaps her fingers four times. Then she looks like she's thinking some more. "Gee, this is hard," she says. "Try, Amanda. Really think. You can do it. I'm transmitting as hard as I can."

I look at her as though the light is coming to me very slowly. "Is the word 'dog'?"

Nelson is scowling from me to her.

She opens the piece of paper with the word "dog" written on it.

Nelson is going from suspicious to begrudgingly amazed. "How'd you do that?"

"By tapping into the psychic power of the universe," Cynthia declares. "We'll soon be able to read all thoughts, any thoughts."

"That's witchcraft, you know," Nelson avows.

Cynthia just laughs. "Oh, Nelson," she says. "You're a funny kid." Then she sits, looking out the window. We are each silent for a long while.

It's as though something has to come together between us. But then Nelson begins, "Well, one thing for sure, even if Spook didn't get Bucky . . . No matter who did . . ." His voice is lowered to a whisper that only the three of us can hear. "Even if it's true what you said about Lander this morning you better not go up there in the woods. All that stuff happened a long time ago, but no one knows who this picture guy is."

Cynthia looks at him and smiles. Then she looks out of the window and sighs. Finally she agrees. "Yeah, I know." She sounds reluctant.

"You want to go and get more pictures, don't you?" I ask her.

She glances at me and blushes. It's as though her eyes don't know where to look, so she looks out the window again.

I'm embarrassed. It's all way too personal. We're all silent for a while until Nelson changes the subject. "When was the last time you talked to Lander about all that stuff?"

Cynthia has been off, far away, and she looks confused. "I never talked to Lander about the pictures. I only told you two about them."

"No," Nelson says. "I mean the other, about Bucky."

"Oh." She sighs, and a look of pain settles upon her face. "A while ago."

"Well, maybe you should talk to him about it again."

I look at Nelson and shake my head. "No, she shouldn't. I disagree. He might hurt her! He could even . . . kill her!"

Cynthia is shocked. "Oh, no! He wouldn't. He has never been mean to me. And Tom and Jarret do stuff all the time. Like, last night he was watching baseball on TV and Jarret wanted to watch that dumb wrestling. You know, where they fake that they're really hurting each other?"

We nod.

"So when Lander went into the kitchen during a commercial, Tom tied a piece of string to the TV cord and put it under the rug. Then, after Lander came in and sat down again and was watching, Jarret jerked the string and pulled the TV cord out. Tom says, 'Oh no, the TV's broken.'

"So, Lander got up and went outside. Then they plugged it in and turned on what they wanted to watch. Only they didn't wait long enough to plug it in, and Lander heard it and came in and found the string. He didn't do anything to them."

"I'd guess he'd kill them," Nelson says.

"No," Cynthia says. "He only hurts himself. I'm afraid he'll . . . kill himself!"

Kill himself! I feel as though I've been sucked into a horrible, swirling whirlpool.

Nelson gets up, and it's obvious that he's going to leave. But before he opens the door he leans over and whispers to Cynthia, "We gotta go. But, remember, don't go up there. And don't . . . do anything. We have to think about this a lot more."

I leave with him, and when we're away from Cynthia's house Nelson breathes out in a tone of dread, "This is really serious!"

I nod in complete agreement. The images of Lander and the tree and Bucky and the snake have filled my brain. Nelson and I separate in silence to go to supper.

After supper everyone comes out again to play hide-and-seek. For the rest of the evening Nelson and I don't talk to each other. It's like we're afraid to talk because there's so much we have to think about that we need a lot of time without words. We even need a long time without thinking.

Still, as much as I try to keep them away, thoughts are continually coming. And I can tell it's the same with Nelson. Every now and then our eyes meet, even though we try not to look at each other.

After a while we start planning the circus some more. Tom and Jarret want to be tigers who get loose and eat everyone in the middle of the gymnastics act. Elinore says they can't, because she's the gymnastic act. Nelson says, "If you guys are tigers and you start to eat everyone, then I'll be an elephant that comes in and stomps both of you to death."

We're all arguing when Lander walks out of his house. No one except Nelson and I even notices him. We exchange glances, and then quickly don't look at each other.

CHAPTER SEVEN

The next morning we go with the rest of the kids to the woods, and everything is different. Now, Nelson and I and Elinore decide things equally. Actually, the way it is, is Elinore and I think up things to do and Nelson says, "Oh, that's good," or, "I like that," and whatever he likes we do.

All the littler kids gather around while we design the morning, and they look from Nelson to me to Elinore until it's settled. A few of them even try to come up with stuff, too.

We're waiting for them to stop arguing, and Nelson says, "I asked Dad, there were horses at the beach. They weren't imaginary."

Elinore laughs, "Horses! At the beach!"

"Maybe it was like *Misty*," I say to her. "That book . . . ?"

"Yeah, you read that book," she insists. "That's where you got it."

Annette's trying to get us to listen to her. "I want to have a 'making a stupid face' contest," she shouts.

Elinore gives her this withering look and mutters, "Okay, Annette, we're having one. You win."

After lunch, in the hot, sit-around time, Nelson and I go to Cynthia's. Elinore's on her porch watching us, and I can practically see steam coming out of her ears. She's furious.

We settle into Cynthia's tiny room, and it's as though we're taking our positions. Cynthia doesn't even seem to be aware that we're there. She's just sitting on her bed, staring into space.

"I been thinking," Nelson begins. "Lander . . ."

Cynthia interrupts with a huge sigh, "Lander was only eleven, and the snake . . . It wasn't poisonous. It was just a garter snake. He didn't mean to keep Bucky in there, but the storm came so fast."

I look at her and then away. She's talking about things that I don't want to hear, so I change the subject. "I wish we could go swimming. We might be going to the beach." I'm rearranging my body so that I'm upside down with my head on the floor, my knees on her bed, and my feet in the air.

Cynthia glances at me, and then she just sits looking out the window. "I've never been to the ocean."

"Never?" I push up on one hand to look at her in surprise. She's shaking her head. Nelson's frowning at me.

"You should go," I tell her. "But go to mine. It's beautiful, with rocks and big, puffy blue flowers. It's perfect. You'd love it there."

"Mine has horses," Nelson says.

Cynthia looks confused. "You go to different oceans?"

"Yeah," Nelson says.

From me, "Each one's different. I go where there are rocks and flowers and fog. Nelson goes where there are horses, and Elinore goes where there's like a fair, with a boardwalk and rides and stuff. Every one's different, but it's all the same ocean."

"I've only imagined it." Cynthia sighs.

"Well, you'd love it," I tell her. "Be sure to imagine water that's always moving and that goes out until there's just sky."

"It's nice with horses, too," Nelson says stubbornly.

"I know I'd love it," Cynthia says. "But all I can think of now is Lander."

She's looking at her hands, and her voice catches when she says, "He was walking over to get Bucky out when the lightning hit, and it almost killed him! He thought God was aiming at him and had just missed that time. But that He would keep on trying until He got him. He was so scared."

"Did you talk to Lander some more about it?" Nelson asks.

Cynthia shakes her head. "No. I was thinking about it last night . . ."

"You should ask him about it again."

She looks at Nelson as though he's not just a kid talking, but someone who's making a lot of sense, and she needs to think about what he's saying. "He only talks about it when he's drunk. If I ask him when he's sober, he might not even remember telling me about it."

Later, when we're alone, I say to Nelson, "Can you believe

this! It's so horrible! That poor little kid in the refrigerator, can you imagine!" It's evening, and Nelson and I are sitting on the bridge abutment staring down into the stream that goes under the road. "And, another thing, refrigerators don't have locks. If someone put me in a refrigerator, I'd just push on the door and get out. What did Lander do, tie the door shut so Bucky couldn't get out?"

Nelson just looks at me. "You don't know much about old refrigerators, Amanda. They aren't like refrigerators are now. The old ones had latches. The one on Grandma Spicer's back porch has latches, and if someone put you in there you couldn't get out until someone let you out."

I'm thinking of the frightened child, alone. "Lander's the most awful, horrible person who ever lived!"

Nelson is making marks on the cement with a stick. "Yeah," he says softly.

"Everyone thought Spook Wade did it, but all the time it was that disgusting Lander. Spook didn't do anything. He didn't have anything to do with it."

Nelson glances up at me. "Well, he's still terrible."

"Why?" I ask. "Maybe he isn't."

Nelson declares quickly, with great conviction, "He's terrible, Amanda. Don't never think he isn't."

"Why? How do you know?"

He seems shocked, as though I'm saying I might really think the world could be flat. "Because he never comes out."

I'm beginning to realize that my picture of Spook is changing. Nelson still sees him the same, the way everyone always has, and I'm trying to explain to him. "But he does come out! He's the man I saw! He's the one who draws pictures for

Cynthia! It might be that he's not terrible at all. He could just be like Aunt Sally says, different and shy or something."

Nelson is shaking his head stubbornly. "Spook's dangerous, Amanda. If he isn't weird, why didn't he go to school and stuff? Why doesn't he just, like, drive a car and go to work?"

"Aunt Sally says he used to sneak out. She says he came out at night when his mother was asleep. Maybe he's just starting to come out again. Aunt Sally says his mother's weird."

"Well, if his mother's weird, he's weird."

I'm tired of arguing with him. "Chad and Jessie are weird."

Nelson laughs. "Yeah, see what I mean? You're weird, they're weird."

I'm thinking of shoving him into the stream, but instead I just say, "I saw Spook and you didn't. He isn't weird."

Nelson and I begin going to see Cynthia every afternoon. While all the other kids are playing cards or watching TV or reading because it's too hot to be outside, we're in Cynthia's room. The Kennedys don't have air-conditioning, but we go there anyway, because it seems like we just have to. We have to see Cynthia every day.

A lot of days we don't even talk about Lander or Bucky. We just sit with her and talk about everything else. Like, Cynthia asks, "Did you ever notice that everyone is like someone on *Gilligan's Island?*"

Nelson looks surprised, but then he shakes his head. "Nah, that isn't so. Know why? There are mean people on the earth but there are no mean people on *Gilligan's Island.*"

"They just don't show their mean side on the show," Cynthia declares, "but each of them has one."

Nelson isn't convinced. "A kid couldn't be like Mr. Howell."

"Sure he could," Cynthia says. "Or a combination. A person could be half Maryanne and half The Professor. You could even be like three or four or all of them. It doesn't matter if you're a man or a woman or a kid."

Nelson asks her for a piece of paper and a pencil and he starts to make a chart of people we know. Then he fills in who is like which one of the characters.

We agree that I'm a combination of four people. I'm The Professor and Mr. Howell and Gilligan and Maryanne.

Cynthia is Maryanne and The Professor with just little touches of Ginger and Mrs. Howell. She doesn't have any of Gilligan.

We all agree that Nelson is Gilligan, the most. He's also some of The Professor. But when we tell him he's also some of Maryanne, he won't write that down. He doesn't want any of the women written down for him, even if he is.

We work on the chart until we agree about everyone. To make it easier we put down codes for the names, like TP for The Professor, MRH for Mr. Howell, G for Gilligan. When we're out and we see someone, like Jarret, we can just say to each other, MRH and GN—that's Ginger.

Then, one afternoon Cynthia starts talking about Lander again. "He could hardly get free of the branches. He said he never heard Bucky after the lightning hit. He wouldn't have just left him there to die alone. He would've gotten someone if he thought he was alive."

Off in the distance thunder is rumbling. I hear it, and I try to imagine the worst storm ever—lightning, thunder crashing, rain that comes in heavy sheets of water that flood everything.

"I have to talk to Lander about it," she says. "I know I do." She seems to be almost talking to herself, as though we're just there to absorb the sound of her voice when it comes out. But we don't care, because we know she needs us.

"It's just that it's so . . . I think I have to talk to him about it. I'm going to, tonight."

The wind outside is beginning to come in small gusts, and Cynthia's tiny room is rapidly growing darker. "Guess we better go before it rains," Nelson says.

Outside, the gusts of wind are picking things up and swirling them around. My hair is whipping into my eyes. I speak into the wind. "Cynthia thinks that kid was dead after the tree fell on the refrigerator. Do you?"

"Yeah," Nelson answers.

"But maybe he wasn't. What if he was just knocked out, and then he became conscious again but Lander was gone? What if he was . . . just sort of crushed in there, and he was screaming, but there was no one to hear him, and he had to die alone? What if it took a long time?"

We're bracing ourselves against the wind. Nelson is considering. He takes a long time to answer. But then he says with conviction, "If the refrigerator was crushed, then Bucky was crushed."

A garbage can comes bucketing along, the wind is rolling it crazily toward us. Suddenly I see a dust devil. Except that Nelson exclaims, "Hey, look, a whirlwind!"

"It's a dust devil."

He looks at me and laughs. "A dust devil? Who ever heard it called that?"

I feel as though I'm a thousand miles from home. Here, there are terrible secrets, secrets about crushed children. Here even something as simple and ordinary as a dust devil is a whirlwind. I'm lost. I'm an alien in a strange land. We separate and go to our different houses.

The storm comes crashing violently through the clearing. Elinore and I are in the living room. I'm sitting in a chair in the middle of the room, but Elinore's on the love seat by the window. After a really loud crash of thunder I say to her, "Lightning can reach in and get you if you sit by a window."

She rolls her eyes, but when the next lightning comes, with thunder practically at the same time, Elinore quickly gets up and pulls the love seat over to the inside wall.

Uncle Cliff is at home and he calls out to Aunt Sally, "Get out of that kitchen until this storm is over." Then he begins to tell us about the storms he's seen on the sea while he was in the navy. I love to hear about the storms and the sea. I tell him that I love looking at the ocean. I love everything about the sea. He looks at me with this funny smile.

Aunt Sally says, "It would be nice if we could go to the beach, Cliff."

He nods. "Umm. My schedule's awfully tight."

"Amanda's never seen the boardwalk," Elinore informs them. "She hasn't seen anything, and if her parents move to Minnesota, she'll be a zillion miles from the ocean and she'll never get there. She never even went deep sea fishing or jet skiing or anything."

Aunt Sally looks at me. "You went to Maine, didn't you? Or was that Nantucket?"

"Both."

Elinore rolls her eyes. "There's nothing but rocks where she went."

"Nelson says there were horses on the beach where he went," I tell Aunt Sally.

"Oh, yes," she says. "They went to Assateague Island, south of here. There are horses there."

Elinore and I just look at each other. Then we both exclaim together, "Horses!" But after "horses," I add, "Wow!"

After, "horses," Elinore says, "Yuck!"

"Jack, at the base, is camping there with his family," Uncle Cliff says. "I'd like to see that place. Maybe if my schedule opens up . . ."

Elinore and I just look at each other, and then we jump up and hook our elbows together and hop around in a circle, each of us holding one of our feet up and hopping on one leg so that we'd fall over if we weren't holding each other up.

Later, in bed Elinore says, "We have to say, 'Beach,' at least ten times each day. Like at breakfast we'll say, 'I ate this at the beach.'"

I nod. "Or, we could pretend to find some sand in our shoes and say as we dump it into the trash, 'This is just like when I got sand in my shoes at the beach!'"

She starts coming up with other possibilities. "Let's count them. Remember, it has to be ten times."

"Think it'll work?"

"Of course," she says confidently.

We're both quiet for a long while, and then Elinore says, "I know you and Nelson are doing something. What is it?"

So, she finally has asked. I feel a tremendous glow of satisfaction. And I think that maybe I should tell her. I actually want to for a second, until I remember how she gloated and bossed me around when I first came. I actually consider telling her, but then I realize that telling her would be betraying Cynthia.

"We're not doing anything. We're just talking about poetry."

"Yeah, right," she says. "I don't even slightly believe it." Her voice is dripping with resentment.

The next morning we're awakened by the sounds of Nelson and Uncle Dan's voices. They come over to Aunt Sally's for breakfast when Annette goes to their other grandmother's. When we go down to eat, Aunt Sally is exclaiming, "The first thing I heard was a tremendous crash! It's a wonder the whole garage didn't come down on him, the fool!"

Uncle Dan says, "Well, he was so drunk he could've drowned in a mud puddle. I went over to help his mother get him into the house. She couldn't do anything with him. Lander's definitely living on the edge."

Nelson gives me a stony look. I'm puzzled. He murmurs, "Lander was shouting really loud last night. Didn't you hear it?"

Elinore butts in with, "Your house is closer to the Kennedys' than ours. They're all trash."

"Elinore!" Aunt Sally scolds.

"What was he shouting?" I ask Nelson.

Uncle Dan looks at me. He seems surprised that I care, and then he answers for Nelson, "Oh, he was just swearing. Nothing anyone would want to repeat."

"I'll tell you later," Nelson says.

Uncle Dan looks at him sharply. "Like I said, nothing anyone would repeat."

"It's such a shame," Aunt Sally says. "Lander's going to cause someone a lot of misery one of these days. I wish he'd go somewhere. Why doesn't he join the army?"

"Amanda's always over at the Kennedys'," Elinore says. Her words are on the table in front of us like a stink bomb.

Aunt Sally's eyes go from Elinore to me. "Yes, Amanda. I don't imagine there's anything wrong with Cynthia, but Lander is trouble. Maybe you shouldn't go over there so much. And there are so many nice kids around who are your own age."

When Aunt Sally turns away from us to put the jelly into the refrigerator, I thumb my nose at Elinore. Nelson laughs out loud, and Elinore gives us a spiteful look.

The grass is still wet from the storm when all the kids come out to go to the woods. Nelson and I go with them.

Tom's telling about how he put white pepper on Jarret's vanilla ice cream the night before and it made Jarret choke and gag for an hour.

"That could kill someone," Nelson says.

"Pepper can't kill anyone," Tom declares. "People put it on their food. It's food."

Jarret gives him a punch in the gut. "My throat still hurts, and it could've killed me. It almost did."

"Yeah, there's pepper spray, and that can kill you," I say to Tom. "You could be a murderer and then you'd go to jail."

Tom comes back with, "They don't put kids in jail."

"Yes, they do," Elinore says. "A horrible jail called Juvenile Detention where there are other kids who are bigger, who squash you like a bug every minute just for nothing, or for breathing."

"Sorry, Jarret," Tom says.

Through the whole morning all I can think of is Cynthia and Lander. And I can tell Nelson is thinking about them, too. Long before it's time for lunch I leave alone, and begin to walk back to the clearing.

I'm walking, when suddenly I hear someone and nearly jump out of my skin. But when I look around it's only Nelson. He's grinning, and he says, "Boo!"

I make a face at him. "I thought you were some creep."

He says, "Yeah, well you probably shouldn't go off alone, not with 'What's His Name' around."

We're walking along in silence for a while. Nelson says, "Lander was really nuts last night. I never heard anything like that, not even when Tom put his car up on blocks. He was swearing then, but not like last night."

"What do you mean Tom put his car on blocks?"

Nelson laughs. "That was last summer. Tom got two blocks of wood and jacked Lander's car up, just enough so the wheels didn't touch the ground but not so much that he would notice it. Then, when Lander started it and put it in gear the car wouldn't go because the wheels weren't touching the ground. They're always doing stuff like that."

I'm laughing. "Tom's the worst kid I ever saw."

Nelson asks, "Who's he on *Gilligan's Island?*"

I'm thinking. "He's Mr. Howell. Mr. Howell would have been a brat when he was a kid."

Nelson considers. "Nah. I don't think so. He wasn't a brat."

"Maybe Maryanne. I'm sure she was."

"Nah. You can't make everybody fit a pattern, even if you wish you could."

We're heading for the Kennedys'. When we get to Cynthia's room, we can see that she has been crying. Her eyes look wild. After we're settled she says, "I talked to Lander last night. I know you kids don't need to hear all this. But it's so bad. I can just feel it all getting worse and worse! Lander told me it's all true. Then he went out. He just stormed out. Now I know he'll kill himself!"

Nelson gives a long, low whistle.

"He . . . He feels so horrible. Mom says Lander changed when he was eleven. I don't remember that. I was only four. But she has always said he got different. She says it was like she lost him then. He was her first child, and it was just him until she had me. Then there were Tom and Jarret, and now the little ones, but she says none of us ever were as sweet and loving as Lander before he turned eleven. She should know about this, too. But I don't know how." Cynthia is twisting her rings. "I'm so worried about him."

Suddenly words start coming from me. They just explode from me, and I'm tremendously surprised at them. "Him? What about Bucky? He was the one who died! He was trapped in the refrigerator! Bucky was only a little kid! No matter what kind of little brat he was, he didn't deserve to die. Lander's a monster!"

Nelson nudges me. He's trying to make me stop talking. But I can't. He tries to interrupt, and I still go on.

"Lander's cruel and vicious. He's horrible!" The words just keep coming. They're like throw up.

Cynthia's face is in her hands. Finally Nelson shouts, "Shut up, Amanda!" But I still keep going. I don't stop until there are no more words left that I can think of to describe

Cynthia's brother, and I've been repeating the same ones over and over.

When I finally do stop, Cynthia just whispers, "I know."

Then I'm really ashamed, and I try to apologize, but all I can get out is a mumbled, "I'm sorry, Cynthia." I'm too mad at myself to even say it very loud.

She's looking out the window. "Lander thinks all of those things about himself. He told me so. Still, I don't want him to die. I wish someone could tell me what to do. I just can't be the one to send him to jail, but he's getting worse."

"And all this time everyone thought it was Spook," Nelson says wonderingly. "It's so weird!"

Cynthia looks around like she's hearing something for the first time. "Charles," she says.

He looks at her questioningly.

"His name's not Spook. I asked Mrs. Mead about him, yesterday. We talked for a long time. He's Charles."

"Charles?" Nelson echoes.

"Yes," she says. "Charles."

CHAPTER EIGHT

Nelson and I are on Mrs. Mead's porch. He has really bad hiccups. "I gotta get a drink."

"Why?"

"To stop hic-hiccuping."

"You don't need a drink," I say to him. "What's your favorite kind of bug?"

He just looks at me. It's time for a hiccup, but he's thinking. "Those big, black things. The shiny ones."

"Now you don't have the hiccups. You won't hiccup anymore."

Nelson settles his big, brown eyes upon me, and I can see he's trying to hiccup. There's astonishment on his face.

"You can't hiccup. You're cured."

He looks confused. "What do bugs have to do with it?"

I just look up to the porch roof. "It's a secret." I've been shuffling a deck of cards and I start dealing for 500 rum.

He's about to ask more about hiccups and bugs, but he suddenly says, "Look."

I follow where he's pointing out through the thick grapevines. Cynthia's walking out of the clearing.

"She's going up to where that guy is," Nelson whispers.

I lean close to the vine. "Yeah. She has a pencil and a tablet." My voice is low even though she's too far away to hear. "She's going up there, all right. What an idiot!"

Nelson looks around at me, then agrees, "Yeah." He sits back looking thoughtful. "Well, she's up around the age where girls get romantic. She probably likes having some guy giving her pictures 'n stuff."

"I wouldn't!" I exclaim. "A stranger? Is she nuts?"

Nelson grins. "Most girls are." Then he ducks.

Cynthia disappears, and we both say in unison, "Let's follow her."

She's far up ahead by the time we get to the logging road. I say, "We gotta stay off the road or she'll see us."

The leaves are soft and wet from the storm. We're creeping along stealthily from tree to tree as though we're scouts for a hunting expedition. "I hope we see the guy," I whisper.

Nelson gestures toward her. "Bet she does, too. See how she's looking around all the time?"

"Maybe we don't want to see him," I whisper.

Suddenly Nelson exclaims, "Amanda! Behind you! Look out!"

I scream and whirl around.

Nelson's on the ground, laughing hysterically. "Gotcha!" He howls.

Far up ahead Cynthia turns around and looks in our direction.

I step out onto the road so she can see me. I'm too disgusted at Nelson to say anything.

When Cynthia sees it's only us, she walks on, and I begin running until I catch up to her. Nelson dashes up behind us. "Boy, did I get Amanda!"

Cynthia turns off the path, dodging small trees and shrubs. When she gets to a low stump she says, "This is my place." She stoops and brushes leaves and twigs away.

Nelson looks around and whistles, "This is nice!"

The sun has gone, and the air is thick, hot, gray, and sticky, with bugs everywhere. "Are you going to write a poem?" I ask her.

She shakes her head.

I look around. "It's going to rain."

Nelson has a stick and he's digging grubs out from underneath a rotten log that's jammed against a rock. "Wish I had my walkie-talkies," he says. "Then, if anybody sneaked up on us we could each run in a different direction and talk to each other about where he is."

Cynthia is just sitting very quietly on her stump, looking far away. Suddenly I have an inspiration. "Why don't you write to the guy? Write him a letter! You could write it now and leave it here for him!"

She looks up slowly, coming back from her faraway look. "A letter?"

Nelson turns around from over at the rotten log and says, "Yeah. That's a good idea. Write him a letter."

I'm already thinking of what it should say. "Yes, you should tell him . . ."

"Now?" she asks.

Nelson comes over. "Yeah, right now. A letter. Tell him. . . ."

Cynthia hesitates for a second, but then she tears out a piece of paper.

"Write, 'Are you Spook or not?'" Nelson says.

Cynthia is shaking her head. She thinks for a moment, and then she writes, "Dear Man," with a flourish.

"Okay," Nelson says, "now put, 'Are you Spook?'"

"Charles," she says. "But I don't think we ought to ask that."

"Well, geez, that's the most important thing," Nelson says.

"How about . . . Ask him about the pictures," I suggest.

"We know he did that," Nelson says.

Cynthia's pencil is poised above the paper. "I know, I'll write, 'Thank you for the pictures.'"

As soon as she has that down, Nelson says, "Now put, 'Come out, Guy, so we can see you. You're giving us all the creeps, slinking around in the woods like a werewolf.'"

Cynthia has to laugh. "Oh, Nelson," she says, "you're a funny kid." Then she says, "Maybe . . . What do you think of, 'I would like to see you and talk to you?'"

"That's perfect," I tell her.

We read through what she has written so far, then she looks up at us. "That's enough, I think." It's obvious she really wants it to be perfect.

"Maybe it shouldn't be to 'Dear Man,'" I say to her. "How about . . ."

Nelson interrupts with, "'Tall Man?' Or 'Skinny Tall Man?' Or 'Artist?' How about, 'Man who sits in the woods and isn't a logger?'"

"'Dear Friend,'" I say.

Cynthia looks at me appreciatively, and writes, "Dear Friend."

"She still needs to say something else," Nelson says. "Like, 'I know you're Spook Wade and you didn't kill Bucky so you can come out.'"

But Cynthia replies, "It's probably best not to mention Bucky."

All the time we've been there talking, we've also been looking around and listening. Nelson calls out, "Hey, Guy, come and get this letter. It's for you."

"Shush!" Cynthia says quickly. "He's shy. You'll scare him."

Nelson is still walking around staring into the woods in different places as though he's expecting to suddenly see someone.

Cynthia reads the final version:

Dear Friend,

Thanks for the pictures. I would like to
see you and talk to you.

Cynthia

We're all satisfied with it, and I'm especially proud of my contribution, "Dear Friend."

A big drop of rain plops down on my nose. In the distance there's thunder. "I can't leave it here if it's going to rain," Cynthia says. She sounds disappointed.

Nelson looks around, then walks over to the big rock by the stump where he was digging grubs. Grunting and turning red in the face he lifts the rock and carries it over to the stump. "Here, put this over it. There. Rain won't touch it under there, but you can still see it."

Cynthia carefully places the letter under the rock where it's sheltered.

Then all three of us dash out onto the path and run back to the clearing with rain coming more and more quickly until it's pouring.

We head for Mrs. Mead's porch at top speed, and when we get there I take one swing and Cynthia gets the other. Nelson sits on the doorstep.

He says to Cynthia, "Thinking about bugs can make you stop hiccuping."

She isn't really listening. An ant is crawling across the porch. He points to it and then comes out with this hugely loud, fake hiccup.

Cynthia gestures toward the house. "Don't be so loud, you'll bother Mrs. Mead."

"Maybe she doesn't have to hear," Nelson says. "Maybe she can read your mind, too, just like Amanda can. You better watch what you think, Cynthia, or you could transmit thoughts to her."

He's serious. Cynthia and I both nearly suffocate trying not to laugh out loud, but then we just give up and laugh anyway. Nelson looks at us, disgusted.

When we can talk again I gesture toward the house. "She's always on the phone."

"I know," Cynthia responds in a low voice. "She's talking to her sister."

"Spook's Mommy!" Nelson whispers loudly.

"I just can't believe she's related to him," I say. "What would she be, his aunt?"

Cynthia nods. "Yes, she's his mother's sister."

"That's why she never believed all the stuff about him and Bucky," Nelson says.

"Poor lady!" Cynthia is shaking her head. "Bucky was her only child." Tears come to her eyes.

I nudge Nelson with my foot, and he looks around. When he sees the tears, he glances away and begins to hum softly. Tears make Nelson nervous.

For a long while the only sounds that we hear are the swings creaking, the steady rain, and Mrs. Mead's voice coming from somewhere deep in the house.

"She should know," Cynthia says, gesturing toward the house. "It isn't right that she doesn't." In her tone there is dread.

"Her?" Nelson looks around at her, shocked.

"Yes. More than anyone she should know what happened." On Cynthia's face there is a terrible sadness. "Bucky was all she had."

Nelson looks like he's afraid to take a breath. "If you tell anybody anything, Lander will go to jail. He might even go to the electric chair."

Cynthia looks at him. Her expression is tortured, and she nods, but then she says, "He . . . Lander . . ." She closes her eyes, and it's like there are sobs going through her body but she's not making a sound.

Nelson gets up and begins to lunge about the porch making air tackles. He's in the middle of a particularly spastic one when Cynthia says, "I'm going to write to Mrs. Mead, too. A letter, like the other one. It won't say anything about Lander, but it'll tell her what happened. It'll be from, 'Anonymous.'" Her voice is hushed and she's speaking rapidly, as though she's trying to convince herself to do it before she changes her mind.

Nelson doesn't say anything, but I can practically feel the thought, 'No!' coming from him. He stops making air tackles and begins walking back and forth. He's actually pacing.

Another letter? This one to a mother about her lost child! I can't even think about it. I'm thinking of getting up and leaving, except that I know I won't.

The three of us are there on the porch, and there is some kind of electricity that is crackling among us.

Cynthia picks up her pen and holds it poised over the paper.

Nelson stops pacing and comes to stand in front of her like he's thinking of preventing her from writing. But, after a few seconds he begins to pace again, more slowly.

From the other side of the porch he pulls the words from himself almost unwillingly, "It might be okay."

Cynthia begins to write. "Dear Mrs. Mead," then a long pause follows.

Responding to the silence, Nelson offers in a whisper that we can barely hear, "Spook Wade didn't kill Bucky?"

She nods and writes that.

The letter to Mrs. Mead is harder to write than the "Dear Friend" one, and there are a lot more versions before it's done. There are heaps of torn-up tablet paper piled beside Cynthia on the swing.

Finally, there are two complete versions, but we can't decide which one is best. The first one says:

Dear Mrs. Mead,

Charles Wade didn't kill Bucky. He was locked in a refrigerator at the dump by someone. A big tree killed him. We are sorry.

Anonymous

The second one says:

Dear Mrs. Mead,

Bucky is in a refrigerator at the dump with a big tree on top of it that crushed it. This letter is from the person who put him there to clear his conscience and that is not your nephew Charles.

Anonymous

Nelson likes the first one and Cynthia says she prefers the second. I can't decide.

We discuss them for a while, and pick the first one. But then we think that it might make her so sad to read the word "killed," that she'll have a heart attack. So we choose the second one.

After it's decided, we talk about how she probably has been thinking for ten years that Bucky was kidnapped by some fabulously rich couple who will die and give him all their money and he'll come home some day, rich and famous. After we talk about that for a while, we think maybe we shouldn't tell her anything.

Cynthia finally says, "It'd be nice for Mrs. Mead to have a

dream like that, but even if she has it, I don't think she can believe it much anymore."

While Nelson and Cynthia are talking I'm thinking ahead, I'm thinking of when Mrs. Mead is actually holding the letter and reading it. I say to them, "We have to always be her friends."

Nelson looks around like, why?

"Because," I tell him, "once she gets this letter she won't have any hope. We have to be like her children to her, and give her presents on her birthday and send cards and stuff. She's a nice lady." He nods.

"I'll put the letter under her door tonight," Cynthia says. "I'll wait till everyone else is asleep."

Nelson says, "It'll have to be really late or someone'll catch you. If you want to stay awake just put thumbtacks all around you on the bed and then you'll be afraid to go to sleep because you'll roll on them, so you'll stay awake. That's what I do when I want to stay awake. It really works."

"I won't sleep," Cynthia replies. "I don't think I'll ever be able to sleep again."

CHAPTER NINE

My mind is so full. Two people will be getting letters. That night when I go to bed I want to think about Cynthia going out to deliver the letters, but Elinore wants to talk about our "going to the beach" campaign.

"We have to do ten or it won't work," she says. "We only did seven today."

"Why ten? Seven's a lucky number, or eleven. I think we have to do either seven or eleven."

"Eleven then," she says. "The more we do it the better."

"I was talking to Aunt Sally today and I said to her, 'Those big, puffy blue flowers in front of Cynthia's house are like the ones we saw at the beach.'"

Elinore says, "Yeah, I heard that one, but you only did two. I got in five."

"I only heard you do three."

"You didn't go along to the store with us. When we were there, I asked her if we have suntan lotion that's strong enough for the beach. And then a little while later I asked her if we could go parasailing if we went to the beach."

"What did she say about parasailing?"

"Definitely not."

Even when Elinore finally gets quiet, I can't sleep. I keep thinking of Cynthia creeping out into the night. She'll wait until it's way late. Then she'll slip out, and maybe it'll be so dark she'll stumble. But eventually she'll find her way to Mrs. Mead's porch. Then she'll tiptoe up onto the porch and shove the letter under the door.

I'm imagining all kinds of things—Mrs. Mead getting up to go to the bathroom, hearing a noise, going into her kitchen and catching Cynthia shoving the letter under the door. I even imagine a lion that has escaped from the circus, coming up and grabbing her while she's out in the dark. Or, Lander coming home just when she's going over there and running over her.

Even if none of these things happen, and she survives the night, the next morning Mrs. Mead will come out of her house after she has opened the letter, and she'll be screaming and crying.

Then someone will go to the dump and find Bucky's body, and the police will come and Cynthia and Nelson and I will have to act surprised so no one knows we know anything.

For a long time I'm tortured with thinking of what'll happen. But when the rain gets so heavy it sounds as though it's pounding down from the sky I finally fall asleep.

The next morning I think I'm still dreaming the rain, but when I get really awake it's still raining. The air in the bedroom is damp and gray. For a moment I don't remember anything, but then it comes back. The letters, both of them, and all of the thinking about what's the right thing to do. While I'm dressing all I can think of is the letters.

After breakfast Nelson and I dash across the clearing through slippery, spattering mud. We run up onto the Kennedys' porch, hurriedly wipe our shoes on the mat, and then go in. We nod awkwardly at Cynthia's mother and then race up to Cynthia's room.

She's making her bed. Seeing our excited, expectant expressions she says wearily, "I . . . I didn't do it. I have to think about it some more."

When I hear that I'm actually just a little disappointed. But Nelson doesn't seem surprised.

I don't say anything about it. Instead, I tell them about our beach campaign, and Cynthia and Nelson start giving me questions and comments that have the word, "beach" in them. I get a piece of tablet paper, number it, and write them all down. When we're finished, there are thirty-five. Elinore and I can memorize them and then come out with them whenever there's a place where they fit.

Later, when he and I are alone I say to Nelson, "I stayed awake all night, practically, thinking about Cynthia delivering that letter."

"I didn't," he says. "I knew she wouldn't."

"Why?" I look around at him. "Why wouldn't she?"

He looks thoughtful. "The letter to that man in the woods is one thing, but this one . . ." We're on Mrs. Mead's porch. Nelson puts down a Monopoly game and starts counting out the money.

"It was her idea. I can't figure out why she didn't do it."

"Because of Lander."

"She's the one who wanted to."

"Yeah, but this is different."

Later that day when we go in for lunch, Aunt Sally says, "Amanda, I know you can't stay in the house all the time, but must you drag in so much mud? I could plant potatoes in the dining room, and you have wet clothes hanging on all the racks. They're dripping everywhere."

Elinore makes a face at me and then she says to her mother, "Amanda and Nelson are in love and Cynthia's telling them how to have babies." Aunt Sally gives her a sharp look.

I don't even care. But I am interested when Aunt Sally says, "Well, Chad and Jessie won't be gone much longer."

"Did they call?" I ask eagerly.

"No, a letter," Aunt Sally says.

I'm glad. I prefer letters. Their calls are always so short, and they never say anything important. I can tell more from their letters. After all, I don't want to stay in the clearing forever, and what if they aren't doing well? Or, what if they are actually thinking of staying in Minneapolis?

Aunt Sally asks Elinore, "Where is that letter, dear?"

Elinore knows I always want to see their letters. She shoots me a spiteful look, but she only shrugs her shoulders when her mother looks at her.

"It was over by the sewing machine," Aunt Sally says. She's rummaging through the things on the sewing machine. Elinore has hid it, of course, maybe even destroyed it.

I am tremendously enraged. I'll have to depend on Aunt Sally to know what the letter says, and Aunt Sally will forget the most important things. Or, even if she remembers everything, how it's said is important, and the handwriting, and how the letter sits on the page. I even like to hold the letter because it's from them. And Elinore, the simpering idiot, is keeping me from it, keeping me from my parents, whom I haven't seen for what seems like years—almost a lifetime, after all I've been through.

They might be in deep trouble. One of them could have frozen to death—although it's summer where we are, I always imagine Minneapolis covered with three feet of snow with the temperature ten below zero. To Elinore I say sweetly, "Let's go to the bedroom and look at your doll collection while Aunt Sally hunts for the letter."

But Elinore knows that once we're in her room she'll have a terrific fight on her hands, and she just shrugs. "I don't want to."

I whisper, "No matter how long you sit there, when I get you alone I'll beat you up." It's a hollow threat. Although Elinore is one inch shorter than me she's ten pounds heavier. Still, I'll tackle her and get in a lot of good punches.

"Just be patient, wittle Mandums," Elinore whispers. "I'm sure your sweet wittle wetter will turn up one of these years. In an hour or so I may hunt for it, but you'll just have to wait until then."

"Spiteful pig!"

Elinore smiles.

The solution comes in a burst of inspiration. "That letter's important to me. Your things are important to you—your doll collection, your porcelain horses, your games. If I get my letter in the next sixty seconds, none of your things will get accidentally broken. But if my letter doesn't appear in sixty short little seconds, your things will go *pfft*. For every five seconds I have to wait, one more of your things is *pfft!* I snap my fingers so that she can get a real feel for *pfft*.

"You wouldn't dare," she snarls. "I'd come to Stump and break everything in your room. I'd turn your bike into scrap steel."

"You'd like to, but you'll never get a chance. I'll lock all my things in my room when you come. I'll lock my bike in the garage or let one of my friends keep it for me. You'll never wreck my things, but if I don't get my letter—it's only forty seconds now—I'm going to break everything you own. You know how clumsy I am. I'll trip and spill indelible ink on your clothes and your bedspread, your carpet, and your curtains."

Aunt Sally is in the kitchen. Elinore gets up and moves toward the sewing machine. "Jessie's dead. They had an accident. Chad's in the hospital, but they don't think he'll live. Mom didn't want you to know, which is why she put the letter in this magazine where you wouldn't find it. But, if you're so anxious to read it, here it is." She pulls the letter out and drops it on the floor in back of the sewing machine where I have to get down and crawl on my hands and knees to reach it.

I don't believe her, of course. "In my hand, stupid!" Elinore begins to kick the letter out, crumpling and tearing it with each kick. I give a quick glance for Aunt Sally, then stomp on Elinore's bare foot, grab the letter, and run to the bedroom.

Reading it makes up for all the aggravation. Happiness jumps from every page. Chad and Jessie are staying with nice people, and Chad loves the area. But, although Minneapolis is nice, they've decided to return to Stump, and they can't wait to see me. They hope I'm enjoying myself and they love me and miss me. They can be so uplifting.

CHAPTER TEN

The next day Nelson and I slog over to Cynthia's in the heaviest rain yet. The whole clearing is a sea of mud. We're in the house, going through the kitchen, and we have to pass Lander. He glances up at us, and I feel a shiver go through me.

As soon as we're in Cynthia's room, we can see that she has been crying. Nelson looks uncomfortable. He says, like he's trying to get her mind on something else, "I fed my Venus flytrap a horse fly that I caught with my butterfly net. It was huge, and I thought it might get away, so I glued its wings together with Super Glue. If I get another one, want to watch? I'll call you and you can come over. Maybe I'll get one this afternoon."

Cynthia shakes her head. There are rivers of tears running down her face.

Nelson says quietly, "You can't be like this forever. Maybe it's time someone else knew something. Maybe you should deliver the letter."

"Oh, it's so hard!" Cynthia's voice sounds like a wail. "I can talk to you, and I know you kids won't tell, but when I try to think of what to do . . ."

Cynthia is looking from one of us to the other. "It's just . . . everything! I can't stand it!"

Beside me Nelson shudders. Then he says, his voice incredibly somber, "I could deliver the letter. That way you wouldn't be the one."

Cynthia is actually considering it.

Nelson gets up. He looks helpless and upset and almost like he could cry. "I'll do it if you want me to."

She looks up at him, "Yeah, I know." But she's shaking her head. "I just don't know!"

Nelson sits down, pulls out a deck of cards and starts dealing out 500 rum.

"Let's play blackjack instead," Cynthia suggests. "I'm tired of rum."

Nelson looks at her funny but he doesn't say anything.

"Yeah, we could," I say. "But blackjack's math. I don't like doing math unless I have to."

"It's gambling," Nelson says. He sounds shocked.

Cynthia looks surprised. "Oh yeah, I guess it is, if you do it for pennies. Let's do it for good works."

Nelson and I both look blank.

"See, you have these slips of paper," she explains, "with your initials on them, and each one is a 'good work.' So, every time you get one, the person whose initial is on it has to do a good work for you. Like they have to tie your shoe if you hand them a piece of paper with your initials on it and say, 'Please tie my shoe.' Or they have to lend you their bike pump, or something."

Nelson looks interested. "If I get enough of them, can I get you guys to take out the trash for me?"

Cynthia grins. "Yes, but you won't. I can clean up with blackjack. You'll end up hanging wash for me."

"Ah, I bet." Nelson makes a face, and we begin playing.

Soon Cynthia has a huge pile of "good works" in front of her.

"I knew I'd hate this game," Nelson says.

Cynthia laughs. "Wonder what I'll do while you hang wash for me. Maybe file my nails."

Nelson is looking stubborn. "I'm not hanging your wash. Maybe—I could deliver your letter to Mrs. Mead." Cynthia just looks at him. He says quickly, "Or maybe not."

"I wonder if the man in the woods got his letter." Cynthia sighs.

There is continuous rain for the next four days. Every day the kids from the clearing all slog from one house to the other to play endless games and watch TV. The second afternoon I say to Nelson, "Let's astound everyone with our ability to read minds."

He just glares at me.

"No, I'll tell you the secret. First someone picks a little word. Something with three letters. Like . . . 'eat.' Then for every vowel, a, e, i, o, or u, you snap your fingers—once for 'a,' twice for 'e,' three times for 'i,' four times for 'o,' and five times for 'u.' Got that?"

He is still looking irritated.

"For the consonants you start sentences with the letters. Like, for 'eat' you'd snap twice for 'e,' then you'd pause and snap once for 'a.' Then you'd say something like, 'Too hard! I can't do this. It just wears my brain out.' The 'T' in 'Too' would be the 't' in 'eat.' Got it?"

He's still scowling, but I coax him to practice, and he gets pretty good. Except that he comes up with the word, "fly," and gives me six snaps, and I don't know what he's trying to do.

When we get really good at it, we go around astounding everyone. Elinore can't figure it out. She thinks we're making some kind of letters with our fingers, and she makes us go into separate rooms where we can't see each other, but we still can do it by talking and snapping through the door.

It's fun for a couple of days, but then I tell her how to do it, and she tells Annette, and pretty soon everybody knows.

The endless days of rain make me feel like we're drowning in mud. Nelson and I don't talk, except for games, and we don't go talk to Cynthia.

On the fourth night Elinore and I are in bed as usual, and it seems like we've hardly gotten to sleep when we're awakened by Aunt Sally. She's shaking us and burbling excitedly, "Get up, girls! Dress quickly! The sun is finally going to come up, and we're going to the beach!" Her voice is filled with excitement.

Elinore doesn't want to wake up. "Go away," she mumbles, and when Aunt Sally shakes her she grumbles, "Let me alone."

I'm thrilled. The ocean! We're really going? I love the ocean!

Aunt Sally is rushing around, throwing things into suitcases. "We've got four days! The first night we're going to Jack's camper on Assateague. He called late last night. They had to come home early so they're letting us use it for one night. For the other three days we'll be in a motel on the boardwalk!"

I get Elinore standing, but she's still in her pajamas, sleeping on her feet. Aunt Sally gives her a little shake. "Hurry and get dressed, Elinore!"

To me she says, "Try to get her moving, Amanda. Cliff wants to be halfway there before the traffic picks up. We'll eat breakfast on the road." She's practically breathless.

I start shoving Elinore into her clothes, but while I'm doing it I'm beginning to think—I can't go now! Cynthia! I can't just leave. Lander! Bucky! Mrs. Mead! All of it! The man in the woods and the letters! We can't go now! It isn't the right time.

It isn't even daylight before we're in the car. Elinore's dressed and she looks alive, but she's really still asleep. I'm still thinking, not now!

Out beyond the edge of the clearing there's a glow coming through the trees. It's the summer sun, a great, golden miracle after all the rain. We're leaving.

As we pass Mrs. Mead's house, I feel like there are a lot of little strings attached to me, and they're also attached to that house, tightening and trying to pull me back.

I try to force myself not to think of Mrs. Mead, or her little, lost boy. Or the tragedy of Lander. Or Spook.

Up in the woods there's a letter, if it wasn't destroyed by the rain! Maybe the man found it. Maybe he read it and then what! Maybe he left more pictures there. Or maybe he wrote a letter.

Can it be Spook? And if it isn't, who is it? I mean, Charles. Cynthia is right, he should be called by his real name. Charles—Spook—whoever he is. A man. But if he's not Spook, what is he? Could he be normal? But then why was he ever weird? Could he be weird and then normal again? Was he somehow lost inside of his brain and then he is just trying to get out? Everywhere here there are mysteries and secrets. But we're leaving, leaving them behind.

Aunt Sally and Uncle Cliff don't know about them. And neither does Elinore. I should tell them. I should say, Aunt Sally, Uncle Cliff, there are things you should know.

But they're excited and happy. They don't need to know something that makes them feel bad. A secret you want to know is when there's a big box in the closet that no one can look in until Christmas.

We pass out of the clearing and into the soft, early morning. It's like I'm being pulled away almost against my will. Away from the web of secrets and pain.

CHAPTER ELEVEN

We drive for a long while, stopping for breakfast, and by then Elinore is awake. "We're soon there," Uncle Cliff says.

I say, "I don't believe there are going to be horses."

Elinore says, "I don't believe there isn't going to be a board-walk."

We go over a high bridge. There's a sign, Assateague Island, and then sure enough, there are horses! There are horses standing along the road in little bunches, horses moving through the woods. We're definitely at Nelson's ocean.

There are dunes, hills of sand, and a wide beach. And horses, horses everywhere. Uncle Cliff is searching for the camper. Neither Elinore nor I have ever been camping before, and we're really quiet, taking it all in. "His camper is number . . . Where? Oh, there," Aunt Sally says.

Elinore and I exchange glances. It's a big tent trailer,

already set up, with a large screened-in tent room attached to the front, like a screened-in porch. Inside the tent room there's a table and chairs. The glances we exchange say, "We're staying all night in that!" My glance means, Oh, wow! But I don't think hers means the same.

For the first hour we race around figuring everything out, and then we dash across the wide beach and jump into the ocean. In the afternoon we go crabbing. Then we get canoes and go on the bay. I'm thinking it's probably pretty deep, but Uncle Cliff measures the depth with his paddle and then hops out and teaches us how to clam.

We help Aunt Sally make a salad, and she cooks steak on the grill over a driftwood fire. Then we go and listen to the ranger tell about the creatures of the dunes. He's showing us things we saw all day and telling us about them. When we see them again, they're going to be a lot more familiar.

After the ranger's talk, Elinore and I go in the ocean again, and then we spend the rest of the evening until it's dark somersaulting and rolling down the dunes. Around the campfire after it's dark, we roast marshmallows. All over the campground there are other families gathered around their fires roasting marshmallows. In the darkness beyond the fires we can see the horses moving. They walk in front of cars, and when cars stop they put their heads in the window.

I say, "Wish we could spend all four nights here."

"That would be nice, dear," Aunt Sally says, "but we only have tonight. We'll have to make do with a motel on the boardwalk. I know real walls and a real shower and a real bed are roughing it compared to this, but we'll just have to suffer."

Elinore says, "What's that high, singing kind of sound?"

"Mosquitoes," Uncle Cliff says. "We'd better go in. We'll all be eaten alive."

We're all in bed with only the canvas walls of the camper between us and the Island night, and we're all awake. Looking out through the mesh window I can see the huge, full moon coming up, and always there is the sound of the sea. Suddenly I want to see the moon on the ocean, but there's a dune in the way. "Can I go look? Just for a few minutes?" I plead to Aunt Sally and Uncle Cliff. "I'll be right back. I have to see it!"

Reluctantly they agree, and Elinore and I race out of the camper in the dark, shining the flashlight so we're sure not to step on any horse plops or toe-nibbling dune critters. We race to the top of the dune, and there, spread before us, is the whole ocean, gleaming under the moonlight in constantly moving bands of silver and gold. Oh! I'm thinking. How I wish everyone could see this, especially Cynthia!

When we're back in the tent, Uncle Cliff tells us about sailing, and then we sing, "Tenting Tonight," and go to sleep.

In the middle of the night Elinore awakens me with an elbow jab in the ribs and then she grinds her knee in my back. "Cut it out," I tell her.

She's climbing over me, muttering, "I have to go to the bathroom."

Once I'm awake I realize, so do I. So we both get up and head out to the screened-in porch to the Porta Potti.

It's no longer bright moonlight, and Aunt Sally calls, "Better get a flashlight, girls."

I'm feeling my way, and I mumble, "We can find it." Just

then I run into something. It's big and dark, powerful and alive, and it flings me back to the wall of the camper with a loud snort. I scream, and Elinore screams.

It's a huge creature, and it's moving. The table topples over with a crash. Things are clattering. Uncle Cliff slams out behind us. "What, what is that!"

Aunt Sally shrieks from inside, "What's going on out there?" She shines the flashlight beam out just as the whole screened-in porch collapses upon us. In the beam of light I catch sight of a horse galloping away, its hooves clop, clopping down the road.

Uncle Cliff is getting up, and Elinore's going, "Oh! Oh!"

"A horse!" Uncle Cliff laughs.

"I hate this place," Elinore snarls.

"I itch awful!" I declare.

In the morning we survey the wrecked screen house and the chewed-up food cooler. "He dropped in for a salad." Uncle Cliff laughs. "Wonder what kind of dressing he wanted," he teases.

From inside the tent Elinore announces, "I have mosquito bites all over me."

I'm scratching, and I feel like I'm on fire. "I do, too."

"They're everywhere," Elinore moans. "I hate this. I bet I have more than you."

"Let's count and see who has the most."

Uncle Cliff and Aunt Sally are reassembling the screened room and laughing about the horse being in there. Neither Elinore nor I think it's particularly funny. They didn't run into a huge, living creature in the dark, not knowing what it was.

We're counting. "I have one hundred thirty-six," Elinore says.

"I have one hundred seventy-eight," I tell her. "I thought it was one hundred seventy-four, but I just found four more in my hair."

"Oh, I bet," she scoffs. "You couldn't have one hundred seventy-eight. There wouldn't be any room left for skin."

Aunt Sally and Uncle Cliff are talking to the people in the next camper about the horse.

Elinore has a pen and she's numbering her bites, starting with her toes. "I bet you don't even have as many as I do," she says.

It takes a long while, but, using a mirror eventually I am up to 160 bites. All over me there are 160 bites with numbers beside each of them in blue ink.

Elinore has only gotten to 127, but she says, "The rest of them are in my hair."

We're just finished numbering when Uncle Cliff comes in. He takes one look at us and then just stops and stares. We're covered with bumps and numbers. He looks shocked. Without taking his eyes from us he calls, "Sally, Sally, come in here!"

Aunt Sally comes in, and when she sees us she goes, "What on earth!"

We try to explain, but she's exclaiming, she's going on and on. "It's indelible ink!" She gets cloths and starts scrubbing, which makes all the bites itch at once. She wails, "Those numbers won't come off!"

Uncle Cliff still looks shocked, but the little laugh lines around his eyes are slowly getting deeper, although he looks like he's trying not to let them.

"We have to go into a motel with them looking like that!" Aunt Sally is in despair. "In the city! What will we do? They look like they have some awful disease! They look like they were in some kind of terrible medical experiment! People will . . . be afraid of them! Us! We won't be able to go anywhere! Not to a restaurant! We won't even be able to go out in public! What on earth were you thinking!"

We're looking really humble, but Elinore does manage to say, "She has a lot more than I do."

"It doesn't matter!" Aunt Sally says. "You both look like absolute freaks!"

All the way off the island and into the city we know to be practically invisible. At the motel after we're checked in, Aunt Sally sneaks us up to the room. Then she sends Uncle Cliff out for ten erase sticks and orders us to erase ourselves. We also have to take an antihistamine for the itching.

The boardwalk is fun. My favorite thing is jet skiing. Second is deep sea fishing, mainly because I get eight sea bass. My third favorite is mini go-cart racing.

Elinore says, "This is the real beach." After the rides her favorite thing is "all you can eat crab." I can't imagine why. The pile of crab shells is ten feet high in front of you before you can get enough crab to fill one little corner of your stomach. Elinore likes the challenge of trying to dig a tiny morsel of meat out of each shell.

Aunt Sally won't let us go parasailing. Both Elinore and I plead and plead, but she just refuses and refuses. "You could end up with plates in your skulls like little Marjorie," she says.

"Spook did that to Marjorie!" Elinore exclaims. "She didn't get it parasailing."

"Or a tree ran into her, whatever," Aunt Sally says. "You're not going parasailing."

The whole time we're there I'm trying not to think about Cynthia, or Lander, or Bucky. But, even though I'm actually constantly making the effort to force them out of my mind, there are quiet moments when I can't help them being there.

Too soon the four days are over, and Aunt Sally is hustling us out of the motel and into the car, but I say to her, "Wait a minute. I have to go and say good-bye to the sea." Then, before she can tell me to forget it, I run up the street and across the boardwalk.

I'm not really saying, "Good-bye." I'm just imprinting the ocean on my mind. Its size. The way it goes out forever, clear to the sky. The movement. So it's a part of me, and stays with me while a whole year passes. Then we're in the car, leaving, going away.

Inside I have a feeling of sadness, just a little at first. But as we go it keeps growing. The farther we go, mile after mile it gets bigger, until after a long, long while it's so huge and overwhelming that I know it's really more like dread. The more we go, the worse I feel.

I'm thinking that it's because we're leaving the sea, and there'll be at least a whole year before I get back. By then I'll be twelve. Or maybe I won't get back in a year and I'll be even older, so old that I'll be completely different. Maybe as old as Cynthia. But when it's time for something to happen, like leaving, there's nothing you can do.

We're driving straight through, and we've been on the road for a long time. I've been kind of sleeping, but not really, because a kite stick is poking my leg, and if I move away from it I'm so tight against the cooler that my arm goes numb. Suddenly the word, "Accident," comes from Uncle Cliff.

I sit up to see. We're almost at the clearing, and on the road ahead of us there's an ambulance, a firetruck, and cars. A lot of people are standing around.

"Who?" Aunt Sally asks. Anyone on that road is probably someone they know.

I recognize the car at the same time Uncle Cliff says, "Lander." He doesn't sound shocked or surprised.

We approach slowly. The car is almost wrapped around a tree, and there are Kennedys standing everywhere.

Aunt Sally stares and then she turns to us and says to us, "Don't look, girls." She even tries to block our view with her hand, but I bob my head out of her reach and stick my head out the window.

Cynthia is ten feet away. She's sitting on the road, screaming, and she's covered with blood. Lander is lying beside her, his head cradled in her lap, and she's leaning over him. She reaches down to touch his head. Then she pulls her hand back and begins to rock, her face twisted with pain.

I try to call out to her. I want to say her name, but the only thing that comes out is a gasp!

Aunt Sally hasn't seen Cynthia, but she's intensely irritated. "Now you'll have nightmares, Amanda," she scolds. "Will you never listen!"

I'm in shock, and I mutter to myself, "It's because he killed Bucky!"

Uncle Cliff is motioned through, and we drive on. After we've pulled up to the house and are getting out of the car, Aunt Sally and Uncle Cliff give me a peculiar look.

Later, when we're getting ready for bed Aunt Sally says, "Amanda, what did you mean about Lander killing Bucky?"

I'm exhausted and sick from what I've seen, and besides I had four cotton candies that day. "I didn't mean anything," I tell her. Then I throw up all over the floor.

As she cleans the floor Aunt Sally says, "You ought to be more careful about what you say, Amanda. Especially . . . Well, poor Lander! Dan just called. They couldn't save him."

I wonder if she saw him, and I feel sick all over again, just thinking about it.

Aunt Sally is going on. "He wasn't much, but it's not good to sully the memory of the dead—and especially for something he didn't even do. Cynthia seems to be your friend, and she'd be very hurt to hear you accuse her brother of killing little Bucky." She's going on a lot more, but I'm drifting off to sleep.

CHAPTER TWELVE

The next morning I'm awakened by the brilliant sun shining into my eyes. From the kitchen I hear Aunt Sally saying cheerfully, "Oh, Dan, I tell you it was wonderful at the beach! Why didn't you tell us those horses were such scavengers? They almost ate our whole cooler. Amanda and Elinore went out to the Porta Potti in the dark and came face-to-face with a horse. It snorted and tossed its head at them. Can you imagine how loud they screamed in the dark, and they were flailing around and knocking each other over! I mean, to suddenly confront a huge animal and see those big teeth and eyes and not know what it was!"

Uncle Dan's chuckling.

"But, all in all, the only thing really wrong with the whole vacation," Aunt Sally says, "is that it ended too soon. Isn't it awful about Lander! How're they taking it over there?"

I get up and hurry to get dressed. I'm bumping into Elinore. We go down to the kitchen and slide in behind the table.

Aunt Sally is pouring coffee, and Uncle Dan and Nelson are sitting across from us. Uncle Cliff shoves the toast plate toward them, and it seems like it's going to be the same as a lot of other mornings with everyone sitting around eating and talking.

But Nelson shoots me a significant look, and Uncle Dan's eyes settle on me. I scrunch down in my seat. Uncle Dan has never looked straight at me before in my whole life.

Aunt Sally sits down to eat. But then she and Uncle Cliff glance at Uncle Dan, and they see him staring. They follow his eyes, and soon all three of them are looking straight at me.

I'm immediately hyper, and I'm imagining them all suddenly standing up, leaning across the table until they're towering above me and accusing me of some great crime—Bucky's murder, maybe, or even Lander's death. It doesn't make much sense, but . . . Nelson reads my mind. "Everybody knows everything, Amanda."

Elinore's eyes race around the table and then back to Nelson. She practically screams, "Knows what?"

"Elinore!" Aunt Sally scolds her for being so loud. Then she looks at Uncle Dan. "Knows what, Dan?"

Uncle Dan speaks slowly, like Nelson, and it takes him a while. But he tells them everything. Three days after we left, Mrs. Mead found an anonymous letter inside her front door. It informed her that Bucky had died in an abandoned refrigerator on the old dump. When she found it, she came crying and puzzled to him.

He thought it was a cruel prank at first. But after thinking about it he decided to go up to the dump to look, and he and Nelson had met the loggers. The six of them had found the skeleton, all that remained of Bucky.

Uncle Cliff is staring at me, and by the time Uncle Dan is halfway through, Elinore is staring, too. With her quick mind Elinore already knows who wrote the letter.

I'm feeling extremely uncomfortable. Elinore's looking at Nelson, too.

"Oh, poor little Bucky!" Aunt Sally exclaims. "How did it happen?"

"Lander," Uncle Dan answers.

"Lander?" The word echoes from each of them.

Then Uncle Dan tells the rest. At first Aunt Sally and Uncle Cliff and Elinore just stare at him. In everyone's mind there is the little boy at the moment of death, the frightened child alone.

"Well, Lander got what he deserved, then," Aunt Sally says.

"Oh, Sally," Uncle Dan says, "he suffered a lot. He had the Devil on his back for all those years. I don't think he had a moment's peace after it happened.

"After we found Bucky—I don't know how I began to suspect . . . Nelson didn't tell me." Uncle Dan throws Nelson a thoughtful glance. "I just guessed. I went over to the Kennedys' and asked Lander if he wanted to go to the police station with me to talk about Bucky, and he said he did, mild and quiet.

"These kids here sent the note—Nelson and Cynthia and Amanda. I guess it was just time for it to come out."

"Cynthia?" Aunt Sally is shocked. Then she looks at Nelson and me. "And you two?"

I nod but my eyes are averted. I'm not sure how I'll be punished for meddling in this, but I'm sure some punishment will come. I just wish I could melt away, become invisible or something, maybe get away with saying I didn't know anything about it and didn't have anything to do with it.

Elinore is extremely agitated. "How did Cynthia know?"

Nelson fixes her with a leaden stare. "Lander told her. It was horrible, Elinore. Not a game." He looks at her like she's a gnat.

"Mrs. Mead's a great lady," Uncle Dan proclaims. "The first thing she did after she found out was go over to the Kennedys and tell Lander that she forgave him." Both Aunt Sally and Uncle Cliff's mouths fall open.

"But Lander couldn't accept it. The police let him go, and Mrs. Mead let him go. But he couldn't let himself go. He packed and said he was going away forever. I guess no one'll ever know why he came back last night. He never made it, poor soul."

Uncle Cliff nods slowly.

"The funeral for Bucky will be Tuesday at one o'clock. Lander's will be at two-thirty. I'm preaching both."

Aunt Sally is shocked. "Dan! You can't preach over Lander. Not when he . . ." She shakes her head.

Nelson motions for me to go with him, and I slide away from the table. Maybe, with so much to talk about, and the funerals, they won't get around to punishing me until my parents get back. But I know that punishment will come. Jessie won't approve of my being involved in sending anonymous letters to widows telling them about their dead children. She'll say it's inappropriate.

Outside Nelson says resentfully, "I wish I could've gone to the beach." He's kicking stones. We're walking toward the Kennedys'.

I look around to see if there's anyone to hear. "Who put the letter under Mrs. Mead's door, you or Cynthia?"

"Cynthia. She didn't tell me she was going to do it. We didn't talk after you left. One night she just did it."

I hesitate, but I have to know. "Was it horrible when Mrs. Mead found out?"

"Yeah," Nelson answers.

I don't push for details.

After a while he says, "I didn't tell anybody—about Lander or any of the rest. Dad just figured it out. He saw us all together a lot before the letter, but that wasn't how he knew. He told me he had suspected Lander a long time before that, like for years, but there just wasn't anything specific. He said he always knew Lander had some heavy burden to carry."

"Wonder why no one ever found Bucky before."

Nelson considers. "Maybe they just figured if he was out there in the woods somewhere he'd be easier to find."

"Did Cynthia . . . Did she ever get anything from the man in the woods?"

Nelson shakes his head. "Cynthia's only thinking about Lander. Don't ask her anything. If you do she'll just cry and cry."

We're on the Kennedys' porch. Inside there are a lot of adults standing around crying, and on the floor there are babies crying. Tom and Jarret aren't there, but then they never are. What is going to be unusual is that Lander won't be there. He'll never be there again.

As we knock on the door the thought flashes through my mind that Cynthia's mother might come to answer it and see us and then come out and hit us. I don't know why I think that, but I get prepared to run.

Her mother does come. But when she sees us all she says is, "Cynthia ain't here." She does give me a penetrating look, and she has almost never looked at me before.

I breathe a sigh of relief as we walk away.

When we're pretty far away I ask Nelson, "Is Cynthia's mother mad at Cynthia or us?"

His answer is careful. "No, I don't think so. Everybody is too busy crying to be mad now. They will be a lot more mad later on."

"Nelson?" I stop walking and look at him. "Do you think Lander is dead because of us?"

He kicks the dirt with his toe and looks off to the trees at the edge of the clearing. He never answers.

Nelson and I see Cynthia out walking with Tom and Jarret later, in the afternoon. For some reason we're hesitant about going over to talk with her, but when she sees us she leaves them and comes toward us. The three of us go and sit under the apple tree.

Elinore, seeing us joined together again, starts a game of catch with Tom and Jarret. She's trying to edge close enough to hear what we're saying, but no one can hear anything with Tom and Jarret around.

"I'm so sorry about Lander," I begin. The ever-near spring of wetness starts to fill Cynthia's eyes.

I'm trying to think of some more comforting things to say

when Cynthia comes out with, "I went up to the woods this morning, up where I always go."

On the other side of her I hear Nelson suck in his breath.

"I was crying so hard. I was screaming and banging my head on the stump . . . He put his hand on my shoulder."

"Cynthia!" we both shriek.

"I . . . I heard him. I wanted to stop screaming, but I couldn't."

I think, will she never stop crying? Can someone die from crying?

"Even when he put his hand on my shoulder, I was still screaming."

"What did he do?" Nelson asks.

"Well, it was just that way for a long time, and then when I couldn't scream anymore he sat down. He said his name was Charles, and he asked me what was wrong."

"Spook!" Nelson and I both exclaim.

"Yes, I guess I always thought it might be him. I told him about Lander. I told him how Lander had suffered for so long. And I told him that no one will ever care about him, except Mother and me."

My mind is racing, but neither Nelson nor I say anything. We just sit, stunned.

Then after a long pause Nelson comes out with, "I care." We both look at him. "You said no one cares, well I do." Cynthia and I still aren't sure what he means. "About Lander—You said no one cares about him except you and your mother." He's speaking slowly, as though he has just discovered a package, and he doesn't know what's inside of it, but he's unwrapping it and is surprised at what it contains.

As soon as I understand what he means I say to Cynthia, "Me, too. I care. I care, too."

Nelson goes on, "And God, and Dad. Dad says God loves Lander as much as he loves Bucky."

Cynthia is trying to smile through her tears. "Your dad told me that yesterday. But why did Lander have to die! I wrote the letter to save him!"

Nelson and I don't answer. We don't know, either. All we know is that we'll have to think about it for a long, long time.

EPILOGUE

Somehow I managed to avoid being punished.

Everyone went to both funerals because Mrs. Mead said they should. Bucky's little snow-white casket was closed, and I tried to imagine his clean, little white bones lying in there, with the skull on one end and the feet on the other. I hope they hadn't just piled them in, any old way.

Uncle Dan said that Bucky had died in terror, but that he was now in a place where there is peace that passes all understanding. He said that Bucky was surrounded by a joy that would never end, and that he was enveloped by a love so strong it couldn't be measured. Uncle Dan said that Bucky's last moments of pain and terror on earth were obliterated by the great, expansive rewards of eternity.

Lander's casket was large and black, and it wasn't opened, either. Aunt Sally said they couldn't have his casket open because, as she put it, he wasn't "presentable." I knew for a fact how unpresentable he was.

Uncle Dan said that God held Lander's soul in the palm of his hand, and that Christ had died for everyone's sins, no matter how great. I spent all of Lander's funeral trying not to think of blood coming out of him and getting on the beautiful satin inside the casket.

When we got to the cemetery after Lander's funeral, Bucky was already buried. Mrs. Mead came over and hugged Mrs. Kennedy. When all of the people from the clearing saw that, they came and hugged her, too. I knew right then that Nelson was right, Mrs. Mead was a great lady. She could have been mean to the Kennedys, but she found a better way to be.

After the funerals Chad and Jessie came back, and I turned twelve. We were back in Stump together again, the way we were supposed to be.

We visited the clearing often. It didn't happen all at once, but Cynthia and Mrs. Mead helped Charles Wade come out of his mental prison. His mother went away for treatment, and Mrs. Mead arranged for him to come and live with her. After that he was always around.

I heard Tom and Jarret call to him one afternoon, "Hey, Spook!" They were hoping he'd do something weird.

But all he did was answer, "Yeah?"

And they just said, "Oh, nothin'."

Charles was always intense, remote, and dignified, and he never made small talk. I overheard Aunt Sally and Uncle Dan talking about him. "He was never autistic," Aunt Sally said.

"That's the thing no one understood. His mother was mentally ill, and the atmosphere he grew up in—well, it just wasn't normal. How could he escape not having problems? But when he could find a way to be normal he did."

"Yes, it was gradual and painful," Uncle Dan says, "but he made it."

"That year when he was caught going into people's homes," Aunt Sally added thoughtfully, "maybe that's what he was trying to do, find out what was normal so he could be normal, too. What a tragedy if he had never been able to manage, and without Cynthia and Dolly Mead I don't believe he ever would have succeeded."

Uncle Dan shook his head. "What a wretched childhood he must have had!"

Cynthia and I, with a lot of help from Nelson, made him popular by telling everyone what a great artist he was.

He always looked at Cynthia like she was an angel, and when he looked at her that way she looked like one. In the evenings they would be on Mrs. Mead's porch with Charles drawing, Cynthia reading, and Mrs. Mead playing the dulcimer. When she plucked the strings a quiet, gentle sound filled the clearing.

Mrs. Mead taught Cynthia to be a lady. The whole clearing learned a lot from her. One person can make such a difference.

The years passed, but that summer in the clearing always, ever after, seemed like a stream that had been flooding and doing a lot of damage. It had caught us in its swift, wild current. But when the flood was over, and the stream was back in its banks everyone could see that it had washed the clearing clean.